CRITCHLOW.

G 13

"JUST GOING TO EAT THAT SLIP—GET IT AWAY!"

Page 123

Frontispiece

JACK FRERE
OF THE PARATROOPS

BY

MAJOR J. T. GORMAN

Author of "The Road to Mandalay"
"Gorilla Gold" &c.

Frontispiece by M. B. Critchlow

BLACKIE & SON LIMITED
LONDON AND GLASGOW

Printed in Great Britain by Blackie & Son, Ltd., Glasgow

Jack Frere of the Paratroops

CHAPTER I

Mr. Brown

Ticket-holders for London jostled each other in the subway, snatched newspapers from the bookstall and rushed for their trains, scowling at the tall, broad-shouldered lad who stood foursquare in the middle of the platform, his suitcase at his feet, rereading the official letter which he had torn open with a reckless disregard of the War Economy labels plastering the envelope.

But, for all the notice he took of his surroundings, the boy might have been a scarecrow in the centre of a field of chattering starlings.

He was far too much absorbed in his occupation, seeing in imagination scene after scene of battle and adventure following each other on the narrow margins of the type-written sheet, dazzling and blurred, in the manner of those words and figures of a film " trailer " flickering across the screen.

World news, just for the moment, did not exist, although only an hour earlier, before the post came, he had been eagerly scanning the newspaper columns for the latest reports about the Battle of Britain. Now those headlines, in memory, ran into one another meaninglessly, like rows of telegraph poles seen from an express train.

It was quite an unpretentious page of typewriting, under

the printed heading " War Office ", this new leaf in his life which he was turning, literally, at that moment.

Just a brief and formal letter which told John Drummond Frere that he had been appointed to a commission in His Majesty's Land Forces and gazetted as 2nd Lieutenant to the Royal Westshire Regiment, dated 25th August, 1940.

" I am also directed to instruct you to report to the 1st Battalion of your unit, stationed at Southron Bay, Sussex, on 28th August. I am, Sir, Your obedient servant. . . ." it ended baldly.

They took up very little space, those few lines of rather faint typing, considering how tremendously important they were.

2nd Lieutenant John Drummond Frere flushed up to the roots of his thick thatch of fair hair, then, recovering his sense of humour, grinned widely at his own momentary feeling of disappointment.

Unimportant-looking was it? Had he expected the announcement to be in letters of gold, or set up in red-inked type?

" Ass !" he apostrophized himself scornfully, but his grey eyes were still alight and eager as they restudied the words.

John Frere, Jack to his friends, had had a good many such thrills during almost twenty years of life. His school-days were punctuated with them in memory: Cricket and Rugger caps; the day he scored that goal in the big match; the proud moment when his essay on the handling of mechanized forces in action had received a special prize and warm commendation from a famous and beloved Royal Field Marshal; the extra awards for proficiency in German and French—but he deserved very little personal credit for *them*.

Yes, all these had been great and outstanding moments in their way, eclipsed by the excitement of that day during the Munich crisis when he had taken French leave from school to enlist. He wasn't much over seventeen at the time, but, being a big chap, they'd taken him, and the H.M. had been very decent about it. And then a few months later, another grand moment when he'd put up his first stripe.

But each and all were completely overshadowed by the reception of that brief communication telling him that he was a full-blown officer in His Majesty's Land Forces.

And best of all, an officer in the regiment which his father and grandfather had both commanded in turn. Perhaps some day he himself—but at this thought Jack Frere's colour deepened still more. That was something even beyond imagining.

" Dad would be proud," he thought. " And Peter will too."

That name brought the new-made 2nd Lieutenant back to realities and the urgent need to share his news with somebody. There was only one person in the world who would be as much interested and excited as himself, and that was his cousin and hero, Captain Peter Loring.

Thrusting the letter into his pocket, Jack made a dive for the London-bound train which, as he suddenly realized, was just leaving the platform. He could not reach town and Peter's flat too soon, and, after all, his cousin expected him anyhow for part of this week-end. After being badly wounded at Dunkirk and sure of a long spell of sick leave, Peter Loring had taken a flat in London for some months, to get an important and pressing job of work finished quietly, as he told Jack. And he had impressed upon the boy, too, that there would be a room ready for him at this flat, that he must look upon it as his home and headquarters when he came up to town that summer.

" And he absolutely meant it too—good old Peter !" Jack thought. " He's the grandest fellow in the world. There's no one like him."

As the train took on speed, the rhythm of its *chug*-chug-chug-chug rising from a dull piano to a double forte, the lad's thoughts continued to dwell on this redoubtable cousin of his. Although barely ten years his senior, Peter Loring had almost taken the place of father, as well as elder brother, to the shy, lonely schoolboy, whose parents had died in India just before the cousins' first meeting eight years ago, when he had gone to see the lad at his school.

All Jack's pleasantest times after that, in Christmas or summer holidays, had been provided by his cousin; there was no one else to take much interest in his prospects, or his career, except the ancient and dried-up family solicitor who was his guardian, and Mr. Perkins had about as much idea of a modern youngster's requirements as an Egyptian mummy. It was Loring who had insisted on adequate pocket-money and outfits, taken him on a never-to-be-forgotten cruise, and for a whole succession of winter-sporting holidays in Austria when both of them had learnt to speak German like natives.

The train, after speeding contemptuously past several halts and minor stopping-places, here pulled up at a large station in a condescending manner and interrupted the course of Jack's own personal train of thought.

A peremptory whistle, a shrill escape of steam, and they were off once more, dropping into the steady *chug*-chug-chug again, passing through fields and woods, gold in the late summer sunshine.

Jack leant back and returned once more to the pleasant contemplation of his cousin.

" What a soldier ! With a D.S.O. won at Dunkirk—and it *ought* to have been a V.C.," Jack commented inwardly.

A captain in the Royal Regiment of Artillery and not only a gunner but an inventor into the bargain, tremendously good at the maths and geometry and dynamics which had almost floored Jack himself in every one of his exams. Jolly good thing soldiering consisted of other things as well, or it would be a poor look-out for his own future career in the army!

He rather wished he understood those matters better though: he'd have liked to be able to follow Peter's descriptions of these inventions of his a bit more intelligently. As it was, the details of the contraptions meant simply nothing to him, just strings of figures and calculations which might as well have been medical prescriptions for all he knew to the contrary, silly ignorant fool that he was.

A new tank gun was the latest of these inventions, the one he was working on at the moment, something light and easily manipulated, but with a tremendous range.

Some new idea for the actual propellant, too, in a solidified form—looked rather like huge jelly squares, Jack thought, when Peter showed him samples.

But the projectiles themselves fired by this weapon were *the* important part of the invention. Not anything beastly and deadly like a super-explosive or poison-gas, but a combination of chemicals, which had an extraordinary effect on the most solid metals, simply melted them away— what was the word?—disintegrated them.

Peter had told him any amount about it all only last time they met, in that sort of eager gasping way he always spoke, quite a trick of his own. It was to be the wonder of the world, that new projectile and the gun that fired it, when they were perfected.

Here was London, though, and Jack put all thoughts of inventions behind him in the echoing bustle at Victoria

Station. He pushed through the crowds and found a taxi-cab to take him to the large block of flats where Peter Loring lived.

Reaching Lamorna Mansions, he was soon running breathlessly up the stairs towards his cousin's front door, on the top floor of the building.

Just as he reached the landing, that front door opened and Peter Loring himself came out with a companion, so hurriedly that Jack was almost knocked backwards down the stairs.

" Sorry, old chap," Loring spoke hurriedly in his usual breathless way. " I can't stop to talk to you now—got an urgent appointment. Back to-night. Richards will look after you."

He passed quickly on, leaving Jack to lean against the wall, feeling like a collapsed barrage balloon. But as the stranger paused close beside him, with an apologetic smile before following Peter, the boy's attention was arrested. For here was someone who could not be disregarded, even although for an instant he had seemed to merge into the brown-panelled background of the corridor and become almost invisible—noticeably unnoticeable, in fact.

Now, as he moved forward, the same impression remained, for he was dressed entirely in brown, with a perfection of detail that was almost effeminate. His hair, eye-brows and small moustache were brown too, like a horse-chestnut in gloss and colour. Only his short thick lashes were of a different tint, a deep vivid red, nearly matching the carnation in his buttonhole. They gave his brown eyes an oddly piercing expression.

He bowed towards Jack without speaking, but with a deprecating movement of his long-fingered, beautifully formed hands, and a little shrug or jerk of the right shoulder, not very marked, but oddly characteristic.

This Jack observed during that instantaneous pause before the stranger followed Loring down the long staircase, without in the least realizing the effects of that passing glance upon the future life of himself and others.

For the moment he could only stare after those two vanishing figures, feeling that he had just watched a dream-castle collapse as though built of playing-cards. He had counted so much on telling Peter his news, put such confidence in his warm and understanding sympathy.

No pancake could have felt flatter than 2nd Lieutenant John Drummond Frere as he entered the flat and confronted the only audience left to him, who was polishing a pair of his master's shoes with a perfectly unmoved countenance and a large bone.

The round pale face of Gunner Richards rarely showed any change of expression, even when he spoke of Loring, whom he hero-worshipped almost as wholeheartedly as did Jack himself.

He had first served with Peter in India and become his batman, a post which he had held ever since, to the mutual satisfaction of commander and man. His perpetual faint smile might have made Richards appear fatuous, almost simple-minded, except for the remarkably shrewd glances of the round black eyes.

One of those looks raked Jack's face now, as Richards raised his head, which had been bent concentratedly over his job, in order to answer the boy's questions.

"What's all this fearful hurry about, Richards?" Jack could not altogether conceal the fact that he was annoyed as well as disappointed by his cousin's casual departure.

"Well, we've been in a bit of a rush for weeks now," Richards resumed his boning of the already well-polished leather with slow deliberation. "It's since there's been this question of demonstrating it at the new shadow factory."

" What's that?" Jack demanded irritably.

" Why, don't you *know*, sir?" Richards' air of extreme surprise suggested that Jack had shown ignorance of the existence of the world itself. " The Loring gun *and* its projectiles; the invention the captain's been working on for years past."

" Of course I know everything about that! What's all this shadow-factory business, I mean?" Jack frowned impatiently.

With a deepened air of superior wisdom, as of one who imparts information to the young and ignorant, Richards discoursed of shadow-factories, such as those under the control of Lord Nuffield and other big manufacturers, with plant and machinery for making parts of tanks, guns, aeroplanes and the like matters.

" And there's an idea of testing-out some of the secret gadgets at one of them, sir—connected with *that*——" Richards jerked his head towards the big desk in the window scattered over with books, blue prints, diagrams and several large black-numbered folders.

" D'you mean that's where Captain Loring has gone now?"

" I understand so, Mr. Frere. You see, there's a question about the suitability of the machinery for making some very delicate bit of mechanism in the projectile: the captain had to see a demonstration for himself to make certain about it."

" Even so, I don't quite see why he couldn't have waited for half a minute to greet me," Jack grumbled. " I wouldn't have kept him long."

" Well——" Richards hesitated. " There's the possibility . . . of course, you know, sir, the captain expects that he might be getting a staff job in the Middle East any time now that he's been found medically fit. It naturally makes him want to get the invention business settled before he goes."

"Whew!" Jack whistled, forgetting his own private concerns for a moment. "D'you mean—does Captain Loring really think there's a chance of his going abroad?"

"I gather he hasn't much doubt of it, sir," Richards answered quietly, and settled down once more to his boot-polishing.

"Who was the other chap—that stranger with my cousin?" Jack asked.

"He was closely connected with the factory, I believe, some years ago, Mr. Frere, when it was only a commercial enterprise, motor-car building on a big scale, I understand—a Mr. Brown."

"Brown, eh? Well, of course, that's just what he is. Couldn't be anything else, could he?"

"Eh? Oh, yes, I see, sir." Richards smiled tolerantly as though at a small boy's feeble joke. "Well, it appears that the gentleman has a lot of influence there and takes a great interest in the captain's invention. I suppose that is why he came for him to-day: he brought a message from the authorities at the factory—Well, I'll be blowed!"

Richards stopped abruptly, staring at the desk. His explosive exclamation had made Jack start and stare too.

"What's up——?" he began, but the other interrupted him.

"Excuse me, Mr. Frere, I'd like to make certain—yes, the captain's taken the wrong folder. I was afraid of it."

He gazed at Jack with an air of solemn consternation, which made the boy feel as though he alone was responsible for a world-shaking mistake. He waited in silence for further explanations.

"Yes," Richards resumed. "These black numbered covers hold details of all the captain's inventions—the mortar and projectile file is number 45. Of course, as a rule, they are kept locked up in this metal box, but last night we had out No. 36 to check over another new idea, a water-cooler for use with light automatic rifles—and that's what must have happened.''

" What? Got 'em muddled, eh?" Jack said, as Richards paused dramatically.

" Yes, Mr. Frere. He's taken 36 instead of 45. Dear me! This is a bad business. Comes of being in such a hurry, sir.''

" Ye-es, I suppose so." Jack hesitated, deliberating his own next proceedings. " Well, it's not much use my waiting here at present, is it? Think I'll go out and do some jobs in town and then lunch. Tell the captain, if he's back before I am, that I'll have lunch out. Don't suppose he'll be late.''

However, luncheon came and went and so did tea-time without any word or sign from Peter Loring, as Richards reported. Neither had he come back to the flat when Jack returned there again after dinner and saw that Richards was anxious, even although his imperturbable face showed no actual change of expression.

" I suppose it's no good ringing up that factory place," Jack suggested. " They'd have closed down for the night.''

" They would probably be working night-shifts, sir," Richards answered. " Anyhow, it would be worth while trying: better than doing nothing at all and not knowing what's happened.''

" Why, Richards, you don't think anything's wrong?" Jack said.

" Wouldn't say that, Mr. Frere, but somewhow I don't feel comfortable about it.''

" I should think Captain Loring's quite capable of looking after himself!" Jack laughed.

" Well——" By his dubious air and shaken head Richards showed that he did not entirely agree with this assumption, but he said no more until he had dialled a number and was speaking into the receiver.

" Yes, they *are* working at the factory, sir," he broke off to tell Jack with an air of relief before he listened again. " Yes. . . . I am speaking from Captain Loring's flat in London. . . . Yes, Loring. . . . I wanted to know when the captain left the factory. . . . He was down with you to-day. . . . Yes, I'll wait while you inquire. . . . Thank you."

There was a long pause, while Richards, his ear to the instrument, waited in silence. At last he spoke again.

" Yes . . . yes; no; I think you must be wrong, sir. Captain Loring certainly left here at about 11.30 this morning to go to the factory. . . . A gentleman came for him—a gentleman named Brown. They were travelling down together. He told me so distinctly. . . . Are you absolutely sure, sir? . . . I don't understand it at all. Is that quite certain? . . . Hullo! are you there? . . . They have cut off."

Richards replaced the receiver and stared at Jack with a curious strained look in his eyes which was almost like fear.

" They tell me at the factory that Captain Loring hasn't been down there to-day at all, Mr. Frere," he said slowly. " He wasn't even expected by the staff."

CHAPTER II

The Screen Unscreens

Jack Frere thought it must be about the millionth time that he had replaced the receiver of the telephone instrument on Peter Loring's desk. Dialling, inquiring, taking down messages—a wearing job.

"Peter ought to have invented something to short-circuit all this sort of thing," the boy thought. "It'd have been a jolly sight better than thinking out gadgets for guns that don't get anywhere, or at least, only to wherever the poor old chap is now—and what wouldn't I give to know where that is!"

Everyone seemed to want to get in touch with Peter. There had been at least half a dozen more or less cryptic wires, besides all these telephone messages, from the last of which Jack was just recovering.

"He'd have to be in at least a dozen places at once, it seems to me!" Jack thought hopelessly. "The only thing that's clear is he ought to be *somewhere*, and he isn't. It's no good for me to try to make head or tail of it all."

The latest wire which had just arrived was curtly brief and to the point, however.

"Report A.G.6 War Office in person."

In person! That was just the snag. Jack flung himself into a chair. Peter was wanted in person and Peter couldn't be produced, while to make things worse, Jack himself must join his unit to-morrow, without fail, which didn't give him much time to clear up things.

He was part of the army now, he must move not alone, but as a tiny cog-wheel in that vast machine. Yet what was

the good of all his training, his tests and examinations and
solutions of paper problems if the disappearance of one
British officer proved an unsolvable mystery? For that was
the state of affairs up till now. All his own efforts and those
of Richards had brought them no nearer to discovering
where Peter Loring had gone, from the moment when he
left his flat with the stranger and passed down the stairs
out of Jack's sight, out of his life.

Nobody of the name of Brown was working at the
factory, and no one connected with the firm had been
authorized to fetch Captain Loring on the day in question, or been given any message or any instructions concerning him.

Neither had Jack, in the course of long conversations upon
the telephone, been able to establish the identity of the man
in brown. His description did not answer to that of anybody
employed by the firm at the moment, although, as the
junior partner, who was speaking, said rather impatiently,
they had had so many agents selling their cars all over the
world, that it would be utterly impossible to identify each
of them offhand.

The fact remained that both men had disappeared, literally into the blue—and Jack was left wondering what on
earth he was to do about it.

But now another problem arose—File 45. Richards was
very unwilling to take charge of this, since it contained such
important and secret papers, or to make himself responsible
for its safety. Besides, although Jack was rather hazy on the
question, surely the plans of the gun and the marvellous
projectile were government property, since Peter was working at his invention for the War Office?

This Jack felt was too big a matter for him to decide
alone, but the question was simplified when he examined the
file more closely. A label on the back of it in Peter's own

writing, stated as plainly as if Peter himself had been speaking to his cousin what was to be done.

" This file is the property of His Britannic Majesty's Government. If found, it should be taken to Room 211X, the War Office."

This decided all Jack's doubts. He must in any case go to the War Office, and explain why Loring could not, at the moment, report in person. He would leave the whole difficult business in the hands of the authorities and at the same time deposit the file in Room 211X as directed.

As he walked down Whitehall in the midday sunshine, Jack felt a sense of excitement. Reaching his destination that vague feeling took solid shape.

The War Office! That square grey building, through the doors of which so many famous people had passed, so many great soldiers. It made 2nd Lieutenant John Drummond Frere feel very small and yet someone of importance in the mere fact that he had business at the War House. Inside, there was not quite the silence and dignity, he expected. A good many people hurrying about, inquirers being interviewed by dug-out officers, the ringing of telephone bells.

Jack took his place in one of the groups and, after waiting for half an hour or more, managed to catch the eye of an official, who attacked him, like an old colonel of horse, as to whether he had an appointment and the nature of his inquiry.

He certainly had no appointment—in his own person at any rate, and this led to so many further difficulties in obtaining access to A.G.6 that at last Jack abandoned the attempt and turned to the matter of disposing of the file.

This did not help matters. A demand to be led to Room 211X met with a most chilly response, and the nature of his inquiry, when Jack tried to put it into words, sounded too incredible for official consideration. The difficulty of explaining the situation prevented him from any attempt to catch further eyes, and he began to think that he was doomed to stand disregarded for the rest of his life, or the duration of the war.

He only received attention at last when, on a desperate impulse, he walked over to the desk of the official and asked if he might take his papers across to Downing Street and try to see the Prime Minister himself, or, failing him, the Secretary of State for War.

This was such an astounding suggestion, so much a departure from red-tape procedure, that the telephone was put into action again. How Jack hated the very sound of it— and a conversation in cryptic language, interspersed with mysterious letters and numbers, ensued, resulting after an interminable length of time in something like action.

" After all, they're only doing their duty," the newly appointed officer to His Majesty's service told himself rather unconvincingly, as he straightened up and marched behind a one-armed ex-soldier into a lift, and eventually, into an office with 211X on the door.

Here he met an entirely different atmosphere, one where he became somebody of importance, or rather, perhaps, someone of interest to somebody of importance, drawn by an almost magnetic power towards a desk at the farther side of the room.

Jack found himself looking into a pair of steel-grey eyes set in a face which gave him enough confidence to tell his strange story with assurance, to find that, in the telling, its difficulties and complications became unknotted, each coil rolling off smoothly, only interrupted by questions and suggestions from the quiet figure on the farther side of the desk.

Everything cleared itself surprisingly. It seemed as though he had been making notes, from which to piece together a carefully corrected manuscript, which was certainly not the case.

When he ended, an encouraging voice spoke.

" It's a strange story, but you've told it very well—very well indeed. You cannot have missed much. I will, of course, take charge of this file of your cousin's."

Jack found himself mentally shaking his shoulders, relieved of the heavy weight caused by that old man of the sea of a file. He was just beginning to thank the speaker when the quiet voice addressed him again.

" And now, au revoir. Let me know if you hear anything further: a letter here will always find me—Colonel G. Parker, Room 211X, War Office. I will set the ball rolling and find out what has happened to our friend Captain Loring. Of course, it's a very serious matter, but it may turn out that there is some quite simple explanation. In any case, leave it to me."

All clouds for the moment dispersed, Jack went lightheartedly down the stairs, out into Whitehall once more. He went on through the crowded streets, dodged across to Piccadilly Circus, escaping a taxi or two, and took refuge on the island in the middle. It was too late for shopping or any other odd jobs. While the boy stood there wondering what to do, the influence of that quiet presence at the War Office faded and lost its power a little. Once more, wave upon wave, his worries and anxieties regarding Peter returned, he found himself trying again to imagine what could have happened to his cousin, what the mystery surrounding his disappearance really hid.

His sense of responsibility returned: after all, there were some things one couldn't shift so easily. All very well to say, leave everything to Colonel Parker! Yet Jack could not see anything more to be done, any steps to take, which might lead anywhere.

Straight in front of him, posters and inviting announcements indicated the entrance to one of the big Picture Houses.

and on a sudden impulse Jack crossed towards the doorway.
" Might as well see the show—perhaps it'll stop me
thinking for a bit," he decided. " Ought to have a bit of
a bust-up too, I s'pose, before I join the regiment. Goodness knows when I'll be in town again."

Standing at the pay-box of the cinema, passing on over
the thick soft carpet into the warm darkness, following the
glow-worm torch of the attendant down the sloping alley-
way to his seat, Jack Frere little imagined that he was actually
taking the first of those steps which he had tried and failed
to foresee, standing outside in the Circus—steps which were
to lead him far, into very strange and dangerous places.

From the first the show was disappointing. If there was
a big, outstanding film in the programme that afternoon,
Jack had certainly missed it and come in for a fill-up. The
name was the best part of it. " The Mystery of Kentston
Castle " promised a lot more than it performed, but what
the mystery or its solution was Jack Frere was never to
discover.

There was nothing in the story of the film, as he saw it,
to stop anyone from thinking, to give one anything else to
think about. Deadly boring, that's what it was.

Jack yawned and wondered whether he could possibly sit
it out—all these endless conversations in lawyer's offices
and scenes between some sort of an old squire and his deadly-
dull daughter. Even the fact that it was a colour film did not
improve matters. Looking at it all with a jaundiced eye,
Jack decided that the crude pinks and greens of the fruit-
trees were quite unlike those West-country orchards he had
so often seen in flower round his school.

He began to fidget in his velvet seat; his thoughts wandered to just those persistent worries which he wanted to
avoid for a little while. And then, glancing towards the
screen, something caught his attention, hit him right between

the eyes, to use his own inward description of what happened.

The scene had shifted to a white road under large trees, the ground beneath them dappled with light and shadow, along which a motor car was speeding. Jack, having lost the thread of the narrative, did not know or care who was in it—probably one of those everlasting lawyers.

The film accompanied the movement of the car, until it stopped short before high iron gates, their flanking posts on either side surmounted by pillars, topped with stone lions, flourishing stone flags.

" *Some* baronial hall, eh!" Jack grinned to himself in the darkness. " Is this the mystery castle, I wonder, or—hullo!"

He sat upright, fidgeting and yawning no longer, staring straight in front of him at the screen, watching every movement of one of the figures upon it like a terrier seeing a rat for the first time.

Not the principal personage who had just descended from the car and was handing out the Squire's daughter. Neither of these two interested Jack Frere in the least. But there were half a dozen passers-by, intended to give a natural appearance to the scene, a woman with a couple of children, a boy carrying a basket, a man who stopped, looking at the car./

It was that individual's suit which first caught Jack's eye, a patch of bright brown, which reminded him——

Then he saw the hat, the hair and the clipped moustache, all brown too, and realized that this was not just a question of a reminder or a resemblance, but the man himself, the man he had seen only the day before on the stairs at Lamorna Mansions with his cousin, the very man with whom Peter Loring had so strangely and inexplicably vanished—the man who could tell him what he wanted to know. At this sudden realization Jack started to his feet, then sank back with confusion, feeling that he had almost made himself ridiculous by accosting a mere figure on the screen as though it were real.

The man in brown turned his head, looked straight out of the picture and smiled—mockingly, Jack fancied, as if in derision. Then he walked on, off the film, while the boy longed madly to stop him. Yet even in his disappearance the brown man had made Jack's certainty more certain, by giving that little jerking shrug which he had previously noticed.

Although Jack sat through the rest of the film and waited, with an intentness which missed nothing, for another appearance of the man in brown, he grasped little or nothing of the story. The mystery of Kentston Castle was to remain a secret from him, except that the film's story hid another and a much more important mystery.

At the end he had learnt no more. The one figure he watched for did not reappear, but Jack still remained in his seat, trying to piece things together, to find something constructive, something helpful in what had happened.

He had discovered that the man in brown was some sort of film actor, but what then? It was scarcely to be supposed that he had spirited Loring away to take part in a picture. Nothing seemed to Jack less likely.

The inquiries which he made in the manager's office at the end of the performance did not help much either. The film had been made by one of the smaller American companies when touring England, on a location somewhere in the Midlands just before the war, the manager believed. It was oldish, as films go, some kind of experiment in colour, and the company had gone back to the States long before.

It wouldn't be easy in the circumstances to get in touch even with the principal performers, and as for supers—

" they just walk on, you know—get the job for a guinea a day while the film's being shot, or just those scenes of it. They're not necessarily professional actors at all, simply amateurs. There'd be no way of identifying any particular one in the crowd, I should say—no way possible! Nobody would even bother to register the names of that sort of performer as likely as not. . . . Oh, no trouble at all! Only sorry I can't help you. . . ."

Jack went out into the street with the feeling that he had travelled an immense distance and arrived nowhere. A clue to the stranger's identity had been put into his grasp as though by an absolute miracle of chance, but when he wound it up the end hung loose in his hand, leading to nothing at all, seemingly.

Well, perhaps he'd be able to think things out more clearly in the morning. This whole day had been such a succession of complicated situations that his brain ached. Wearily Jack made his way to Peter's flat to sleep on his problems, after hearing from Richards that there was no news of his cousin.

One job to be done stood out foremost next morning. It led Jack to the War Office to tell Colonel Parker how he had identified the film-super with the man in brown, seen with Peter Loring.

This time the boy was taken straight to Room 211X and once more felt cheered and steadied by the quiet personality of the man behind the big desk.

Colonel Parker listened, nodded, asked a few questions, took a few notes.

" I will make sure that the right people see that film to-day," he observed. " It may be a useful clue."

Jack travelled down to Southron Bay that evening, without hearing more. It was not until some days later that he received a letter from Colonel Parker telling him where their first clue had led—and the knowledge gained was not calculated to reassure any who cared for Peter Loring.

That same afternoon after Jack's second visit to the War Office, two unassuming men, in grey flannel slacks and tweed coats, had chanced to drop in at the cinema off Piccadilly Circus where the " Mystery of Kentston Castle " was being shown. They watched the film through and afterwards made a report—which resulted in the brief communication Jack received at his camp in Sussex from Colonel Parker.

For the pair of unobtrusive individuals from Scotland Yard had recognized the man in brown at once as Max von Kressen, a Nazi agent, quite well known to the authorities in both England and France. Fanatic friend of Hitler, one of the leaders of the Third Reich—this was the man into whose hands Loring had fallen.

CHAPTER III

Men in Brown

There was something strange in the atmosphere, not at once identifiable, when Jack Frere woke at réveillé on his first morning in billets at Southron Bay.

The sounds filling the sea air were familiar enough to him by now, after two years of soldiering.

The Corps of Drums, bent on making sure that no soldier should turn over and have a second five-minute sleep before obeying the command to " rise and shine ", were announcing so loudly how " Little Widow Murphy had a little pig ", that one might have imagined the heads of big drum and side-drums being made from the skin of that same unfortunate quadruped.

The troops themselves added to the concert with their

whistling and singing: bugle-calls impatiently summoned orderly-corporals, words of command tripped up hurrying feet. And far more alluring to the senses than any of these things was the all-pervading smell of breakfast; coffee, bacon, sausages.

And then Jack suddenly realized why he was feeling so strange, so unreal. He had heard all this before as a soldier in the ranks: now, for the first time, he was listening to these early-morning army sounds as an officer—and feeling exactly like a new boy again, in the lowest form at school.

For it really seemed as though he had to relearn everything. Jack never forgot those first hours under the regimental sergeant-major, with his waxed moustache, red face and stupendous word of command. The boy felt just like a bit of chewed string when he had finished that early morning's parade. Afterwards, for the rest of the day—and for many succeeding days as well—it was impossible to sort out any single particular minute one might call one's own.

Orderly-room, guard-mounting, more parades, physical jerks—Jack began to think that the future of the army in action depended on physical jerks—and the R.S.M.'s voice.

There were such an interminable number of little things to remember, and at the back of Jack's mind was always the knowledge that Peter, the only person who really mattered to him, would be hurt and angry if he shirked the smallest detail of his professional job through pre-occupation with what had happened to his cousin.

That stopped him from thinking of it too much, which was perhaps as well, made him work hard and keep his mind occupied with boot-fitting, medical inspection, ration-carrying, inoculation, orders, counter-orders, disorders, all intermingled to make up his duties as a subaltern in His Majesty's service.

He couldn't remember all the details of those first days, Jack found, as, when the third evening came since joining his regiment, he sauntered along the sea-front at Southron Bay waiting with impatient misgiving for the second mess dinner call to sound. It seemed an endless time since the strains of the first had faded away, although, looking at his much-inspected wrist-watch, he found that it was just fifteen minutes, and he had another quarter of an hour to wait before entering the big hotel which housed the mess, to occupy one of the seats of the mighty among his brother officers.

Was he turned out immaculately, as far as battle-dress admitted? He pulled nervously at his tie, straightened and restraightened the lapels of his blouse, tried to adjust the crease of his trousers to an angle align with his boots.

He fingered a much-crumpled card in his pocket, took it out and tried to decipher the writing. The darkness prevented that, but Jack knew the wording by heart, and repeated it over aloud, just to see that he wasn't making a mistake.

" Lieut.-Colonel J. H. A. Watson, O.B.E., and officers of the 1st Battalion The Royal Westshire Regiment request the pleasure of his company to dinner——R.S.V.P. to the Mess President."

That reply! No essay Jack had ever written was so hard to put together, but it had been finished and sent off at last after the war-wasteful destruction of many sheets of notepaper.

Jack looked at his watch again. Only two minutes had gone, and he started to think of his routine duties once more. Inspecting the guard with the adjutant, inspecting the men's meals, visiting the sentries, being halted, challenged to stand and give the countersign—there was still somehow a bit of a thrill in that. Trying to sort the jobs

into order was like picking out tunes on a super-size gramophone record of medleys as it spun round.

And if you stopped the rapid movement carelessly, it
might upset the mechanism.

Mechanism—yes, that's what it had been up till now.
He'd felt mechanized, like the rest of the army. Perhaps a
change was coming, Jack thought, as he came to a standstill and stared out across the invisible strip of shingly
beach, which one knew to be tangled with barbed wire and
tank-traps, at the dense, unbroken blackness of the seas.

Above, the ebony background of the sky was scattered
over with glittering silver points, forming those patterns
called Orion, the Plough, Cassiopeia's Chair, or that silver
dust, so thick along the heavenly highroad, of the Milky
Way.

Behind him, silent, dark, dead, rose the tall frontages and
blank windows of those hotels, boarding-houses and blocks
of luxury flats, once gay and fashionable, blacked-out now
in every sense of the word. All the lights were extinguished,
like those of the bandstand and the pier, which had glittered
so dazzlingly on holiday evenings against a setting of summer
sea, from which had sounded dance-music, voices, laughter.

Now the dark mass of the pier, stretching out seawards,
could only be dimly discerned with that ugly gap midway
along its length, made for defensive purposes.

But those seaward-facing buildings were not all so dead
as they seemed.

Suddenly, from the one-time luxury hotel immediately
behind Jack, a bugle rang out with the notes of " Officers'
Wives have puddings and pies "—and 2nd Lieutenant
Frere realized that the dreaded moment had arrived. He
adjusted his collar and tie for the last time, mounted the
steps, pushed his way through a screened, light-proof
double door, and found himself in the ante-room, thick

with cigarette smoke, with a cheerful hum of voices and laughter.

And, after all, it was just a simple, friendly matter. Jack caught the colonel's eye and paid his respects without difficulty and was already feeling quite at home when the mess-sergeant at the door announced loudly: "Dinner is served, gentlemen, please!"

It was then that the newly-joined 2nd Lieutenant received one of the greatest surprises of his life, concentrated into a glorious and embarrassing moment.

He had dropped back into a modest position in the rear of that straggling procession which made its way to the dining-room. But somehow, by a series of evolutions, twistings and turnings, Jack found himself not, as he had naturally expected, at the extreme foot of the long table, but seated between the commanding officer and the second-in-command and receiving the courteous attention due to some great personage, as the guest of honour.

Listening to the talk around him, once he had recovered his wits, the boy wondered at the way it seemed to wander through all the countries and among all the people in the world. Everyone there appeared to have some story to relate, some recollection, some exciting adventure, some thrill of war or sport.

One day, Jack thought, perhaps he'd be able to make his own contribution to such conversation—although that didn't seem likely to him at the moment. Meanwhile, there were plenty of things to be noted, customs of the mess, although all the fine regimental silver and trophies which would have been displayed in peace-time were stored away for the duration.

One queer thing which struck him was that they didn't drink the King's health—and Jack had been eagerly expecting to hear those famous words of the loyal toast: " Gentlemen—the King!" Queerer still, the Royal Westshires were proud of this omission.

"You see, Frere," the major explained to Jack, "we were excused from Royal health-drinking by George II himself after the Battle of Dettingen—he said the regiment had shown its loyalty so completely by its behaviour there that further proof of it was unnecessary."

So to the lilt of the regimental march "Hail, Smiling Morn" and the stately strains of the "King", Jack's first official mess night came to an end and he went to his billets, well and truly initiated as a Royal Westshireman, beginning to feel at home in the regiment.

Hard work, hard play, both directed to one end—that described Jack's life during the following weeks adequately enough, until a day which again completely changed its direction.

He had heard little or nothing in the meantime concerning Peter. No further communication came from Colonel Parker, and Jack felt himself far too small fry to begin a correspondence with such big fish as departmental heads at the War Office, unless he had something really important or useful to tell them.

Richards wrote two or three times in answer to his letters, and even through the stilted, conventional phrases inscribed in the neat copy-book hand, Jack could plainly read the same anxiety and desperate unhappiness regarding his master which he had seen in the man's eyes after Peter's disappearance.

He had heard nothing from or of Captain Loring, Richards said: he'd begun to think there'd been some fatal accident which didn't get into the papers because of all this war news crowding it out. Otherwise an officer like that couldn't just disappear and nothing said. What did Mr. Frere think?

(G 13)

Mr. Frere did not know what to think, and got no help when he diffidently wrote to Peter's regiment of Royal Horse Artillery. Captain Loring was still absent without leave, came the frigid answer: if there was anything further to communicate, Mr. Frere should hear in due course.

Blind alleys everywhere—and Jack never guessed on the day in question that he was to catch a glimpse, however ugly, of what might be hidden at the end of one of them.

It began with an early awakening from a very vivid dream. He had been drilling a division of infantry in P.T., carrying out a series of evolutions with a strong company of regimental sergeant-majors, he himself acting as their instructor.

A grand example of wishful thinking, but it wouldn't do to lie there indulging in it, when he had to be on parade in less than half an hour. There was no time to waste this morning, for he was to be one of a contingent from the Royal Westshires which was to attend a tank display near a camp some thirty miles from Southron Bay.

The drive in motor-lorries through the downland country-side this fine autumn morning was a demonstration of how beautiful England could be, even in war-time. They passed the great air-station, where Jack and his brother officers had been made free of the R.A.F. mess and were becoming familiar with flying men, their language and machines.

Up and over the guardian bastion of downs and they were roaring down a steep gradient to the plain beyond, and to the vast training-ground which had spread so far beyond its original limits since the outbreak of war. Whitish ribbons of roads ran criss-cross, intersected by the mounds, clusters of trees and shallow valleys which were part of its natural aspect and still further diversified with trenches, shell-holes, sandpits and man-made obstructions of many kinds, examples of camouflage, large excavations for the purpose of housing appearing and disappearing targets.

2

But although they were nearing the scene of action now, no troops, no armoured fighting vehicles were visible: all appeared innocently quiet and peaceful, and Jack might almost have thought that they had mistaken the rendezvous, if it had not been for the gathering crowd of spectators and for the air of tense expectation which spread from them over the whole scene.

When he and his companions had been de-lorried and joined the waiting throng, Jack found those spectators a most interesting study.

Men in brown one and all, there was nevertheless an immense diversity of detail, enlivening the drab ground of the battle-dress cap and blouse. For here were representatives from almost every branch of the British army, every arm of the service, distinguished from each other by a variety of badges, chevrons and rank-marks which were nearly as heraldic in their nature as though they had been worn by the forces who fought at Crécy or Agincourt, bearing the crests of their leaders in war.

Here were men of a Guards battalion, who wore a single eye on their sleeves, an ancient symbol of the Household Brigade. A little group from the Suffolk Regiment showed red and yellow stripes, reproducing the colours of those roses the men of this old regiment wear on Minden Day: others from the Rifle Brigade displayed a narrow black stripe.

Besides this, there were a bewildering variety of beasts and birds, regimental or divisional signs, black cats, scarlet dragons, green gryphons, rhinoceroses—appropriately symbolizing an armoured division—numbers of big and little constellations of stars, with a conspicuous Southern Cross significantly adopted as a kind of monomark by the Southern Command.

Further variety was shown in headgear, the black berets

of the tanks, those of maroon and dark green worn by airborne regiments and commandos respectively, vivid pipings and linings diversifying the caps of gunners, sappers and troopers of various mechanized cavalry regiments.

Staff officers with their red tabs and smartly-dressed girl-chauffeurs: numbers of Home Guards, with yellow flashes on their dun-brown sleeves—all these touches of colour lit up the scene, like small high-lights of history and tradition.

Jack jumped. Suddenly the warm noonday peace, the steady buzz of voices, like loud-toned bees among the thyme, was broken by other sounds, a rising roar, the growling thunder of innumerable engines.

It was a dramatic moment, for it seemed as though tanks, troop-carriers, cars, lorries, armoured fighting vehicles of every kind were rising from the very earth itself, as they emerged from hidden hollows and excavations, from the shadows of hedges and the fringes of woods, where they had been skilfully camouflaged and concealed.

Down from the higher slopes, over the lower, gently undulating ground they came, first swarms of motor-cycles, carrying automatic guns, their riders looking like robots, with their goggles and tall crash helmets. Then " Beave-rettes ", small armoured-cars, nosing along like land torpedo-boats, or rushing forward at fifty miles an hour.

Light tanks, their guns projecting in impudent defiance: then the great battle-cruisers, Covenanters and Crusaders, preceding the heaviest " I " or infantry tanks, Valentines, Churchills, Matildas, like moving fortresses.

There was something immensely impressive, almost terrifying, in the steady advance of these armoured monsters, as they crushed down any obstacles in their way, took trenches and ditches in the relentless drive of their cater-pillar tracks.

The noise was terrific now, a deafening crashing thunder

of engines, tracks and ponderous wheels, grinding over the hard ground. Jack tried to imagine what actual battle conditions would be, when to all this was added the stentorian voices of the guns, the screeches and roaring of dive-bombers, swooping from the sky.

But it couldn't be done: his ears could not fancy a greater din and tumult than this, which stunned and bewildered the senses. He tried to practice concentration, by counting the tanks engaged in the operations. He had reached 400 before the scene abruptly changed. It was as though a button had been pressed by some unseen master-umpire. The great massed formations of tanks and other vehicles broke up, spread out fanwise into smaller groups, individuals.

Moving at top speed and with the same amazing suddenness which had marked their appearance, they now disappeared, speeding into cover, vanishing into folds of the ground, hollows, hidden valleys, copses and sunken lanes.

With incredible quickness, the whole force scattered and the wide contours of the training-ground appeared as blank and empty as before the demonstration began. Almost simultaneously, too, the roar of engines died down, ceased: all was still once more, except for a rising buzz of voices.

" I say, what a wizard show!" Jack burst out, turning towards the little group of his brother-officers, who, as he supposed, were still close to him. But they had all dispersed, unnoticed by Jack in his absorbed interest. Looking round, he could not distinguish where any of them were, and he flushed crimson, as his eager comment on the demonstration met with no response.

Nobody seemed even to have heard it. The groups nearest to Jack were mostly composed of Home Guardsmen, some hundred or more, and most of these appeared to be discussing various knotty points with a good deal of heat and vigour.

Having satisfied himself that his comrades were nowhere near, Jack prepared to go in search of them, for he knew that the lorries were timed to leave on their return journey to Southron Bay in less than half an hour. It would be a nuisance to miss the bus, and Jack began to elbow his way through the crowd of Home Guards when a movement on the part of one of them about fifty yards away caught his eye.

It was nothing much, only a tiny upward jerk of the shoulder. But it was oddly familiar to Jack: he had seen it, or something very like it, twice before, in circumstances which he was not likely to forget. The man's back was turned to him: he must see his face at once, before giving himself time to think how impossible it was, this thing which he imagined.

He sprang forward and touched the brown-sleeved arm. Its owner swung round—and Jack found himself staring straight into the brown, red-lashed eyes of Max von Kressen.

The shock of it, the utter unexpectedness of having his vague suspicion confirmed, took the boy's breath away for an instant. He stared, wondering if he could have been touched by the sun. It was so utterly incredible—the well-known commonplace Home Guard uniform—and the man.

Then his scattered wits seemed to click back into their places and his fingers tightened on the sleeve he still held, as the army slogan flashed into his mind that he who attacks, wins.

" What are you doing here?" he demanded, controlling his voice with an effort. " And where's my cousin, where's Peter Loring? Tell me this instant!"

Jack could have sworn that his first words brought a gleam into the man's eyes, a quick evasive glance. Then those brown eyes became blank as glass marbles, and he shook his head with a slow, countrified movement.

" You be makin' some mistake, sir," he drawled. " I

don't know 'ee. I've never seen 'ee afore, so far as I can think."

" That's a lie—and you know it!" Jack burst out. " You're Max von Kressen, and I'm going to find out where you took Captain Loring."

" Beg pardin', sir, but you do certn'ly be wrong," the other persisted patiently. " I don't know nobody of that name you sez just now. I be Mark Tappacombe of No. 1 Battalion Wilts Home Guard, just come overalong with my mates to see this here tank demonstration. I'll join 'em now if 'ee don't mind. The lorries'll be waitin' to take us home."

He moved away as he spoke, twitching his sleeve from Jack's grip. But the boy strode forward again. It was unthinkable that this man should escape, that he should lose like that the only clue to where Peter was.

" No, you don't!" he ejaculated. " You won't get away from me like that. I'm going to call a military policeman— then we'll see what you have to say."

But even as he spoke, Jack knew that he was talking nonsense, bluffing without the faintest chance of success. For he was bound not to call for help, could not even suggest to the military police or anyone else that von Kressen was an enemy agent who ought to be arrested. Colonel Parker had been most insistent that Jack must not say a word, but leave the whole affair to be tackled by those in authority. It left the boy unable to act, tied and bound by his promises, as he wished von Kressen to be in reality.

He could not put his threat into execution. Realizing this, Jack yet looked round instinctively for assistance of some kind, and the instant of inattention was quite enough for von Kressen. As an eel vanishes into a crevice with lightning speed, so the man in brown disappeared into the crowd of brown men, Home Guards and regular soldiers, who were now making their way towards the parked lorries.

Finding him gone, Jack followed as fast as he could, and began to make hurried inquiries, first of one man, then another. Had they seen—did they know, what had he called himself? Mark Tappacombe? But all the Home Guardsmen he interrogated stared blankly.

No, they didn't know him—never come across the fellow. "But he was here only half a minute ago, I was talking to him," Jack persisted. "He told me he belonged to No. 1 Battalion of the Wilts Home Guard."

"Well, there's a lot of us here comes from that battalion," one man said, taking off his cap and scratching his head thoughtfully. "But I've never heard tell of a Tappacombe in our lot. Look here, though, our adjutant's over there: he'll tell you, for certain sure."

He did—but in no way that was encouraging to Jack. When discovered, after a brisk if exasperating search, the adjutant could only tell the distracted subaltern of the Royal Westshires that there was not and never had been any such man as Mark Tappacombe in the 1st Battalion of the Wilts Home Guard.

Both he and the other Home Guardsmen who gathered round listened with sympathetic interest to Jack's hastily improvised, rather halting, story about Mark Tappacombe knowing a relative of his, whose whereabouts he wanted to discover, and did their best to find him. The man had disappeared, absolutely and completely. Probably by now, after passing through one group after another of the brown men whose uniform had given him all unconsciously such a fine chance of escape, he was far enough away to be at any rate temporarily safe from Jack's inquiries.

The Home Guard adjutant summed up the situation.

"It's an extraordinary example of how easy it is to make a get-away in battle-dress," he said.

There seemed no course for Jack except to rejoin his own contingent, which he managed to do, just in time to take his place in the lorry. He'd made an awful mess of things, he thought drearily: probably mucked up the one and only chance of capturing von Kressen and discovering Peter's whereabouts. And the scoundrel was still free to do any amount of further mischief—that was another horribly serious aspect of the affair.

What on earth would Colonel Parker say or think? For there wasn't any doubt in Jack's mind he must make a full report to the colonel of what had happened, however badly he himself came out of it.

He'd better get to work on it that evening, try to set everything down plainly, in as few words as possible. And Jack, as he went over the notes of the events in his own mind, little imagined how much more was to happen before that day ended, what additions were still to be made to that report of his.

CHAPTER IV

The Voice

For the second time in twelve hours, Jack found himself speeding along the road which led inland over the downs from Southron Bay—and this time speeding was an understatement.

He was seated pillion behind a brother-subaltern upon a motor cycle which was being let out to its utmost capacity. They were on their way to dine at the R.A.F. mess, and Jack's companion insisted that they hadn't too much time.

" My word, Collins, you're overdoing it," Jack expostulated. " My hair was nearly blown off my head at that last bend. Talk about ' How we brought the good news from Ghent to Aix!' "

" Up-to-date version, eh?" Collins grinned back over his shoulder. " But don't forget, young fellow-me-lad, speed's the slogan of the army of to-day, and they do everything at the double. Even we poor old foot-sloggers have had to learn that, with our troop-carriers and platoon trucks."

" 'Spose you're right," Jack said thoughtfully. " Horses aren't quick enough for the R.H.A. and the cavalry nowadays—guns have tractors, quads and dragons, and the other fellows light tanks and armoured cars. No use having striking power if you don't use it quickly—as snakes do."

" Talking like a blinking army textbook, aren't you?" Collins laughed. " Only you haven't mentioned airmen in that speed-saga of yours—and here we are at the 'drome in less time than a fly would take to wink."

It lay under the bluish-grey evening sky, the centre-piece to a very English stretch of landscape. Above the great oval amphitheatre in the dimming sunlight, shimmering-bodied aircraft darted to and fro like dragon-flies, hiding and seeking behind softly woolly balls of cloud.

On the ground, there were fewer signs than might have been expected of the nests of those giant insects. The hangars were so skilfully camouflaged as to be almost unnoticeable: officers' billets hid modestly in the clearings of a wood skirting the airfield, with a certain air of snugness. Lorries and other vehicles covered with netted foliage seemed to form part of tree-land, a telephone lurked in a clump of bushes, while a makeshift kitchen was planted casually on the edge of those surrounding fields, brown, lime-sprinkled, yellow or green in many shades, a patchwork quilt covering the country side.

Yet there were plenty of sights and sounds of activity for those who listened and looked. From behind a thin screen

of trees came the tinkle of metal and tools, where a machine
sat straddled like a patient puppy while aircraftmen tinkered
and jigsawed at a broken wing-tip. A little farther away a
big bomber, somewhat shorn of its majesty, was undergoing
repairs, while the noses of other aircraft peered out inquisi-
tively, as sheltering rabbits might have done, from long
grass and undergrowth.

Only about the labours of the artificers and groundsmen
there was nothing casual: they worked with speed, skill
and concentration, each at his own particular task, near
their bivouacs under the wings of spare machines.

Jack and his companion were joined by a young flight-
lieutenant after handing over their motor cycle. Now, as
they strolled towards the mess-building, the drone of the
weaving, gliding aircraft overhead was drowned by the
louder throb of an approaching machine's engines.

A graceful wide-winged Spitfire planed down to make a
perfect landing and a stampede of running feet, and shouted
orders from the ground-staff escorted the machine to its
hangar.

The pilot, unfastening his crash-helmet as he walked,
passed near the group on their way to the mess and the
flight-lieutenant hailed him.

" Any luck?"

" Not much," he shrugged; " one ME down and a second
possible."

" That chap looked very young," Jack remarked, as the
Spitfire pilot swung off out of hearing.

" Oh, we've younger fellows who're flight-commanders
and squadron-leaders. That's one of our best types—a
pukka wizard. You'll probably meet another to-night who's
barely twenty, but has a big bag to his credit already. His
name's as long as his legs—and that's saying a lot!—Miles
O'Morough-Ryan. *The* O'Morough-Ryan, if you please,

and don't leave out that ' *The* ' or there'll be trouble! But
' Shanks ' is what he's usually called. You'll know him at
sight—he's got the whole map of Ireland on his face."

" Sounds a bit of a freak, eh, Frere?" young Collins
chuckled. " We'll be pleased to meet him, as our Yankee
pals say."

Jack agreed, with a mild sensation of curiosity which he
little knew heralded his introduction to an individual who
was to become another of that strangely assorted company
interested one way or another in the mystery of Captain
Peter Loring.

It was not until after dinner that they actually met. Once
again, Jack had been struck by differences between this
mess and that of the Royal Westshires. This was more
informal, and there were a greater variety of types. A few
senior men, flyers of the last war, well-seasoned and tough-
looking, their outspread wings sheltering two rows of
medal-ribbons, smoked large briar-pipes as if nothing else
in the world mattered. Some still older, inclined to some
degree of corpulency and the joviality which accompanies
it, were old service men with ground jobs.

But the majority there were young, with the keen clean-
cut look of the up-to-the-minute flying-man, wearing, some
of them, D.F.C.s, A.F.C.s, and other ribbons, watchful,
alert youngsters.

Standing out from this mixed assemblage, as he had a
habit of doing from any crowd, was the man with the name
as long as his legs, who was quite easily recognizable from
that description.

At that very first encounter—oddly enough, as he was to
think a little later—Jack felt attracted to Flying-officer
Miles O'Morough-Ryan. Lolling back in an exceedingly
low chair, he gave a first impression of towzled red hair,
many freckles and lazy, half-closed eyes.

Then as he slowly unfolded himself, rose and crossed the room to turn on the wireless, the reason for his nickname became clear. He was very tall, thin and lanky, immensely long-legged, so much so that, as he bent towards the instrument, Jack was reminded of a many-jointed ladder being put up against a wall.

His eyes, although still only half open, had no suggestion of sleepiness about them. They were oddly variable in colour, capable of changing from steel-grey to deep blue, with every intermediate shade imaginable, but at this moment, as he glanced from one face to another, with his fingers on the switch, they held a glint of mocking defiance, as though saying for their owner: " The programme *I* choose on the wireless, you'll like too—or I'll know the reason why!"

And that, as Jack was to discover later, was the attitude towards many things in life of The O'Morough-Ryan.

The nine o'clock news was duly given by an impeccable announcer, followed by a special recording from one of the fronts by an ultra-literary war correspondent and an order concerning the cheese ration.

Abruptly, the self-appointed master of the ceremonies switched off and thrust both hands into his pockets.

" It's too early for that unutterable swine," he remarked. " We'll have to wait a bit to hear what new lies he's broadcasting this evening."

" Can't think why you bother to listen to him, Shanks," another airman remarked. " Not worth poisoning one's ears with pure and simple enemy propaganda like that."

" I don't agree—it's just as well to hear what the brutes are saying," one of the youngest flying men present intervened, to be snubbed rather curtly by an older man.

" That's nonsense, Raikes, you don't eat deadly toadstools, just to see what they taste like."

A rather heated discussion followed, some taking one side, some the other. Above it rose the voice of O'Morough-Ryan.

"I listen just because it's such an extra-abominable case. One wouldn't mind it so much coming from a plain brute of a born Jerry, or even a treasonable rebel of an Irishman like Haw-Haw. It's their job, so to speak. But when it's a matter of one of ourselves, a British officer turned traitor, well——"

"Come, O'Morough-Ryan, there's no actual proof of that surely?" It was a quiet-looking squadron-leader who interposed. "It seems to me we're all too willing to believe anything we hear in the way of tittle-tattle about spying and treason these days—in fact, we're just living on our nerves."

"You're wrong about there being no proof," O'Morough-Ryan's eyes were very wide open now and dark-blue with concentrated indignation and anger. "There's enough and more than enough in my opinion."

"Well, I for one don't believe it," the squadron-leader still spoke with quiet deliberation. "I'm not out to preachify but it puts back the hands of the clock as regards everything English, if we must accept as a fact that we are one of those nations of quislings who'd sell their country for a mess of pottage—or thirty pieces of silver. That's my feeling, anyway."

There was a little buzz of approval and agreement, which seemed to exasperate Flying-officer Miles O'Morough-Ryan. He threw himself back in his chair with a sliding movement and hurled his bomb into the middle of the assembled company with an air of pitying derision for his over-credulous seniors.

"Perhaps I'm more easily convinced, a simple sort of boob—but I have it on the best of authority from a fellow who knew him well and recognized his voice at once that this new announcer from Germany is a fellow called Peter Loring, an ex-gunner captain, who's deserted from his regiment since the war began and——"

The remainder of Shanks' assertion was drowned in a loud chorus of dissent and disapproval half laughing, half angry.

" Rot !" " Rats !" " Pity to repeat that sort of gen——"

" I don't care a hang what anyone else thinks," O'Morough-Ryan's temper was rapidly rising. " I stick to my guns. I absolutely believe myself that this swine who's sold himself to the Boches *is* Loring and——"

" And you are a damned liar !" Jack's voice came clear and loud above all the rest, and Shanks, taken aback for the moment, swivelled round and stared at him in amazement.

" What d'you mean ?" he demanded.

" Exactly what I said—and if you don't withdraw that lying statement, I'll punch your head till you do, you long drink of dirty water !"

There were some expostulations from the company, and Jack found himself sharply reminded by this that he was the guest of the mess, and these other men his hosts.

He flushed crimson, but spoke firmly enough, staring straight at The O'Morough-Ryan. " Gentlemen, I apologize to you all for saying it here—but not for what I said. I stand by that, and I'll repeat it, anywhere or to anybody who dares to call Peter Loring a traitor."

" Oh, you will, will you !" The Irishman was too angry now to care what he said. " You seem to know a lot about this contemptible fellow. Perhaps you're a type of the same kind yourself ?"

" I only wish I was; I'd be proud to think so," Jack answered. " Because Peter's one of the best men who ever lived. . . . He's my cousin, so I ought to be in a position to know if he's a traitor or not."

" You *ought*, certainly," Shanks drawled, as he rose and sauntered towards the door, pausing for an instant to jerk back carelessly over his shoulder. " Sorry and all that, if I've said anything about a near and dear relation to hurt your tenderest feelings. But he's not my cousin—thank goodness!—and I haven't changed my mind about him or what he's doing."

He closed the door behind him, and there was an uncomfortable silence, broken by the squadron-leader.

" I'm sorry for what happened, Frere," he said gravely. " But Shanks is a hot-headed youngster, apt to blurt out things he's sorry for afterwards, when he's in a temper. And, of course, he couldn't know of your connexion with Loring."

" Of course not, sir." Jack spoke quietly, but there was a grimness in his voice which made Collins, standing close beside him, whisper uneasily.

" You won't make a scene here, old chap? It'd be rotten bad form."

" Of course not," Jack repeated, while the others began to talk and laugh again as though trying to wipe out all traces of the unpleasantness. Under cover of the conversation, Jack edged towards the door and went out unobtrusively and unnoticed. A wooden veranda surrounded the mess hut, and here, as he had somehow expected, the boy found The O'Morough-Ryan, perched on the railing, whistling softly under his breath as he gazed up at the moon. He grinned wickedly at sight of Jack.

" I thought you might turn up—to keep that promise of yours," he remarked, and Jack met his glinting glance steadily and with set lips.

" I have," he said. " Come on."

He was pulling off his blouse as he spoke, and Shanks did the same himself, leading the way without further comment to a little clearing among the trees only a short distance from the mess hut, but screened and not overlooked.

" Going to punch my head, aren't you?" the Irishman thrust his chin forward aggressively.

" Unless you withdraw what you said about my cousin, yes!"

" Sez you! Well, why don't you make a start? I'm waiting." The chin was advanced a few more degrees.

" All right. I'll not keep you any longer. Are you ready? Take that then!" The out-thrust chin received what was coming to it.

It was not a matter of tactics or science, that fight. Neither combatant had more than the vaguest ideas of the rudiments of boxing strategy, but both youngsters were thoroughly angry and in grim earnest. As Jack lunged forward again after the first blow, Shanks swerved aside; then they faced each other once more expectantly, fists clenched to charge almost simultaneously, with no formalities or preliminaries by way of introduction.

Shanks's long arms and legs, grotesquely reproduced in black shadow silhouette by the moonlight on the pale, dry turf, were like the thrashing limbs of an octopus reaching out, grasping, efforts which Jack, quicker and more nimble on his feet, evaded, darting this way and that, waiting for a chance to get in under that clumsy reckless guard.

When he managed to do so, his opponent received a blow which sent him backwards, staggering and winded. The luckless Shanks tried to retaliate, but his forward drive was badly aimed and nearly resulted in his falling headlong through losing his balance on the slippery turf.

After that, the fight rapidly degenerated into a mixture of boxing and all-in wrestling, with no rules, rounds or regulations, Queensberry or otherwise. Both evaded blows and clutching movements, both, in turn, received heavy punches. There was plenty of the wildest of wild hitting and missing, as they broke away, dodged and gripped again, with much straining and grunting.

It was rather like a contest between two young bulls, as they stamped and butted, stumbled and came in to the attack again, puffing and almost exhausted, but both equally and doggedly determined not to give in.

Jack paused to wipe away the blood which was trickling down his face from a cut on the forehead, while Shanks, also temporarily out of action, leant against a tree, gasping for breath from a wind-punch. The long-legged Irishman had lost his air of defiant cocksureness, with the gain of a black eye and a disfiguring blue lump on the point of his chin.

When they resumed the fight by a kind of common consent, it had become a ding-dong affair, the blows and parries somewhat lifeless. It would have seemed to an onlooker as though neither youngster could last another minute, and both inwardly knew that this was near the truth and resolved to fall in his tracks before he would admit defeat.

It was with that last despairing effort which sometimes inspires the novice boxer that Jack flung himself forward, and with a pendulum-like swing caught Shanks once more under that aggressive chin and sent him staggering and floundering backwards, while going down himself to sprawl on the ground across his opponent's outstretched legs.

But while the soldier sat up almost at once, the airman remained unconscious, and Jack, still dazed and sick, gazed at him uneasily. Suppose he was dead—there were certain blows that could kill a man outright—what if this had been one of them?

That would be pretty awful.

But even as mixed fear and remorse made Jack drag himself up and pull himself together to investigate, Shanks moved, groaned and opened his eyes.

" Wash' I knock' out?" he inquired thickly. " You jus' wait min'—till I can stan'——"

" You can't," Jack told him, omitting to add that it was very doubtful whether he could either.

" No—don' b'lieve I can," Shanks confessed after a few tense moments, supporting his head on his hands. " Not to-day, anyway. Feel all funny—head gone into a spin."

" You give me best, then?" Jack demanded sternly.

" Yes, confound you—I s'pose so—'sfar as fighting goes," Shanks groaned. " Here, help me up, can't you?"

Jack hastened to give him a hand and to offer him an arm, which, however, The O'Morough-Ryan refused, declaring he could walk and would be perfectly all right directly he'd had a drink. As the two were agreed on this point, they proceeded together towards the mess hut with that end in view, a few yards apart and with as much steadiness as they could assume.

But when the pair were within a few yards of the veranda, Shanks stopped, glaring at Jack suspiciously from his one uninjured and unblackened eye.

" Mind you, even if you did knock me out, I've not changed my opinion," he declared. " You can lick a chap in a fight, but that doesn't jolly well alter what he thinks—and I still think that cousin of yours is a——"

" Don't say it!" Jack broke out fiercely. " Because, if you do, I'll have to knock you down again and——"

He was interrupted in his turn. Suddenly, from inside the mess hut came the sound of a voice upon the wireless. It was a pleasant, ultra-English voice, with a slight, not unattractive breathlessness, a hint of hesitation very characteristic, very unmistakable, and the first words it spoke were startlingly incongruous.

" Germany calling. . . . Germany calling. . . ."

" Good heavens, it's Peter!" Jack gasped, without realizing for an instant what he was saying or what he had admitted.

" There, you've heard: you've allowed it now yourself." Shanks spoke with sullen triumph. " Of course, it's your cousin—*now* will you call me a liar again?"

" Be quiet, can't you? Let me hear what he's saying," Jack muttered desperately, and the other man stood silent, glancing sideways at his companion's face, white and strained in the moonlight, as the pleasant, too-familiar voice went on saying terrible, incredible things with a sneer which was totally unlike the Peter whom Jack knew so well, which sounded as though he had been possessed by a devil.

It hurt almost unbearably to listen, yet he must, he must take it all in, know the very worst.

" It goes without saying that you haven't heard the truth about the air-battle which took place over the Channel to-day," that voice which was Peter's and yet not Peter's went on. " You never do hear one word of truth from any of your lying hypocrites of leaders, your Winston Churchills and Edens, and never will, unless you choose to listen to me, or to one of us over here who know and are not out to deceive you.

" Here are the facts, then, unpleasant, of course—but then war *is* unpleasant, if you take a hand in it yourself and don't expect other people to do all the fighting for you— British fashion!

" This afternoon, twelve ME 110's, escorting a small force of bombers, attacked one of your convoys in the Channel, sinking five or six large vessels and two at least of the convoying destroyers. The exact number of these involved is not yet available, but——"

Here an infuriated comment broke in from one of the airmen.

" The liar! Not a single ship in the convoy was sunk—and only one destroyer slightly damaged! I was there and know!"

The ingratiating microphone voice went on unperturbed.

" The ME's were then attacked in their turn by at least fifty or sixty Spitfires and a succession of dogfights took place over the Channel. Twenty-seven of the R.A.F. fighters crashed into the sea in flames: the rest fled before the Messerschmitts in utter confusion. The victorious Luftwaffe lost only one machine—a fine record for your magnificent Air Force to add to its battle dishonours."

As the mocking voice ceased, there was the sharp click of the wireless switch being turned off, and a clamour of angry voices and comments burst out. When it had died a little, the measured tones of the squadron-leader were audible above the rest.

" What do you expect to hear if you turn on the tap of a lie-factory? Speaking for myself, I'm utterly ashamed of having listened, and I certainly shan't do so again. Good night, boys."

Outside the mess hut, where the late combatants still leant against the veranda rail, Jack spoke stiffly, drawing himself upright and holding out his hand.

" I apologize for calling you a liar, O'Morough-Ryan. Will you shake?"

" That's all right," the other mumbled awkwardly, thrusting out his hand. " It was only a mistake and—and I'm damned sorry about your cousin. It's rotten for you."

" As to that, I don't want you to misunderstand me," Jack went on in the same dull level tones. " You were speaking the truth when you said that was his—Peter's voice. It is. But you were lying, all the same, when you called him a traitor. He's not that—he just couldn't be."

"My word, this is a funny way to apologize!" Shanks broke out angrily. "What the devil d'you mean by it?"

"I can't help it, and I don't know what the explanation may be," Jack said wearily. "But I'm going to find out—somehow. In the meantime, you'll just have to take it from me that the thing *can* be explained."

"I'm not going to then," Shanks declared sulkily. "I said you couldn't convince me by any amount of knocking down—well, you can't! And—and—I withdraw all that business of shaking hands with you. It's not any use pretending to be friends, when we're not."

"Oh, all right!" Jack shrugged his shoulders. "Have it your own way. I don't care."

But when after some difficulty he had discovered Collins and the motor cycle and they were all three on their way back to Southron Bay, Jack found an unreasonable sort of regret lingering at the back of his mind behind all the other more urgent worries and problems the day presented. For he still felt that, in other circumstances, he would have liked to be friends with The O'Morough-Ryan—although, as things were, nothing could be more impossible.

CHAPTER V

In the Dark

If Jack had expected that the carefully-written report to Colonel Parker, describing his encounter with von Kressen and his discovery of the identity of Peter Loring with the broadcaster from Germany, would create an immense sensation, it seemed that he was quite mistaken.

All that he received from the colonel in acknowledgment

was a brief note, to say that inquiries would be set on foot:
no commendation, censure or condolences, although Jack
really could not decide which of these he had thought would
descend upon him.

Regarding the fight with The O'Morough-Ryan, nothing
more happened at all, which was both a relief and a disappointment. Jack certainly had not wanted a court-martial
or court of inquiry, but it gave him rather a flattened-out
sensation when no notice whatever of the affair was taken
by the authorities.

Contradictorily, while hating to hear any criticism of
Peter, it was a comfort to have the chance of defending him
against such attacks. However, no further mention was
made of the matter, and the Royal Westshire Regiment, its
officers and other ranks, settled down to routine duties once
more.

It was on one of these tours of duty that a subaltern
tramped along the dark and deserted sea-front of Southron
Bay, about a week after the tank demonstration, on a night
which could only adequately be described as extremely
dirty in the naval sense of the word.

The young officer was inspecting part of the defences
allotted to the battalion—if anything could truthfully be
described as inspection which took place under conditions
of such dense and complete blackness, that it was impossible
to see more than a few inches in front of one's nose.

Ears had to take the place of eyes, and there were plenty
of sounds to serve as more or less deceptive guides to the
solitary walker.

The sea made its presence and its position known by an
incessant restless movement, the chafing of shingle pushed
backwards and forwards, as though the great ocean monster
stirred uneasily in its hard bed, could not settle quietly
down to sleep. Tiny waves lapped and whispered on the

beach, or against the wooden groynes, a larger one breaking now and again with a splash.

From inland came a softer, more uneven rustling, as a breeze off the downs loaded with fine rain stirred the branches of trees and sent showers of drops pattering to the ground.

"Must be passing near the Marine Park Gardens at that rate," the subaltern thought. "Funny how one can really get an idea of one's whereabouts by listening-out even when it's black like this. S'pose that's how animals manage in the dark. . . . What's that?"

He paused and listened; the sea, too, seemed for the moment to be holding its breath, so that no sound broke the eerie quiet. Yet he could have sworn that he had heard a footfall just before.

It must have been imagination, perhaps the echo of his own steps on some hollow stone. Anyway, he must get on with the job and not begin fancying things. There it was again though. He pulled up short, ears strained, fingers feeling for his revolver.

This time there could be no question of a mistake. Some-one was walking just ahead of him, keeping step roughly, but at a much quicker pace, breaking at intervals almost into a run.

In the wet, misty darkness it was not possible to make out any definite shape, nothing more than an occasional vague uncanny movement.

The young officer took a few almost noiseless steps forward, but simultaneously the hidden figure began running with soft uneven pattering sounds as though on tiptoe, so that the rhythm was broken. Would it be best to challenge at once? No one moving stealthily like that at night in a forbidden area could be up to any good. Perhaps, though, it was wiser to wait, follow, and see or hear where he went.

The subaltern moved quietly forward. After all, it was

possibly some soldier playing the ass, even if that wasn't likely. He'd give whoever it was a chance, anyway, although it might really be his duty just to shout and shoot. . . .

Then the lightly-falling steps suddenly ceased altogether and, at the same moment, the faint blue flicker from a screened torch showed just ahead.

Again the young man stood still. This looked uncommonly like a trap: it called for a very careful advance, which he accordingly made, without switching on his own torch.

He had just made the discovery that the dimmed light came from inside one of the concrete pill-boxes which studded the sea-front at intervals, but were not all manned in the ordinary course, when the glimmer was extinguished.

But the young officer hesitated now no longer. Pulling out his revolver, he reached the pill-box entrance in a few strides and, wisely keeping to one side under cover, spoke into the dark interior.

"Who's there?"

There was no answer, only an almost imperceptible rustling movement.

"If you move, I shall fire!" the officer said sternly.

"You won't, Lieutenant Frere," came a low whisper. "Not when you hear that I have very important news to give you of your cousin, Peter Loring."

Jack recognized von Kressen's voice, although he had only heard it before disguised under a countryman's drawl. He spoke perfect English, with none of the harsh rasping accent so unconvincingly characteristic of the German spies of films and fiction and which would certainly give them away at once in real life.

"So it's you, is it?" he said grimly.

"Presumably it is I—since you appeared to recognize me the other day."

"You mean when you were playing the part of Mark Tappacombe of the Wiltshire Home Guard? Well, if you're so anxious to speak to me, why didn't you take that opportunity instead of running away?" Jack demanded.

"It was rather too public, my dear young friend. You wouldn't have had me tell our secrets to all the world, surely." Von Kressen spoke in a light sneering manner which Jack found intensely irritating.

"Anyway, there's nothing to prevent you from coming outside now to talk," he retorted impatiently.

"Nothing, except the fact that it is a wet and most unpleasant night, which makes conversation far more comfortable under cover. So, since we've got this convenient shelter, why not take advantage of it?"

"I'd rather be out in the open," Jack answered doggedly. "I don't trust you a yard."

"Really, not even if I hand over my revolver to you, as a guarantee of good faith? I'm quite willing to do so—temporarily. Come, we shall get no further, if you won't even meet me half-way!"

"Hand it over, then," Jack said ungraciously. He found it impossible to imitate von Kressen's suavity.

"If you switch on your torch for a moment, you will see that I am actually holding it out to you—no, don't do that! Listen, we mustn't show a light!" The spy's voice changed, roughened, as high above the ceaseless murmur of the sea rose the unearthly wail of sirens.

It was the almost nightly alert, but simultaneously came the broken throb of aircraft engines and the barking of ack-ack guns. Then the whine and crash of a bomb sounded not far away, and Jack felt icy-cold fingers clutching his wrist.

"Come inside," von Kressen muttered. "It's playing the fool to stand out there, risking a shell-splinter."

Knowing the near proximity of one of the anti-aircraft batteries, Jack reluctantly agreed. It would be madness, too, to show a light in these circumstances, and he allowed himself to be drawn inside the pill-box.

A strange setting for the strange conversation which followed. Through the narrow entrance Jack caught glimpses of the sky, the low-hanging wet blanket of cloud lit luridly by gun-flashes, stabbing searchlights, the occasional reddish-orange glow of a parachute flare.

But the interior of the pill-box was pitch-dark: from first to last that night Jack did not catch a glimpse of his companion. He remained only a voice in the blackness.

" I have been waiting nearly a fortnight for the chance of speaking to you alone," von Kressen said. " That is the only thing which brought me to this part of the world."

" You'll scarcely expect me to believe that," Jack said contemptuously.

" It is true, though. For my own sake, yours and Captain Loring's, it was essential that I should have a word with you. . . . Curse those guns! I can scarcely hear myself speak."

" Where is my cousin?" Jack demanded abruptly.

" In Germany."

" I know that. I heard him say so."

" Ah, you listened to one of his broadcasts, I suppose."

" Yes. And I know this too—that somehow you swine have forced him to give them!—have put the words into his mouth. He'd not do it willingly."

" Well, well, I should stick to that belief. I'm sure it must comfort you, whether it is true or not."

" You sneering devil! It is you who are responsible for everything. You kidnapped my cousin, you've made him appear a spy, a deserter, a traitor——"

" Rather waste of time discussing my shortcomings,

isn't it?—even to relieve your feelings. I gather you want to know your cousin's exact whereabouts. I can tell you that—on conditions."

" I can't see that any promises or conditions you make are likely to be anything but meaningless," Jack said bitterly. " You don't suppose I can trust you?"

" It's hard to see how you're to avoid doing so if you want to learn anything at all," von Kressen answered drily. " Still, if you prefer to risk the loss of your cousin's life, rather than enter into any further negotiations with me——"

" What do you mean?" Jack asked fiercely. " What are you hinting at?"

" I am not hinting at all. Merely telling you plainly that Captain Loring is in the greatest possible danger—and that you can almost certainly save him, if you consent to do what I ask."

" How? What is it?"

" I warn you that you won't like my suggestion," von Kressen said.

" It can't be much worse than what's happened already. Go on."

" Well, it concerns a file of papers, one which your cousin fully intended to take with him when he accompanied me on our Continental journey."

" When you carried him off, by force or fraud, you mean, pretending that it was to a British factory where his invention was being tested. I'm absolutely sure he never went with you willingly."

" You're really very well informed." There was a note almost of admiration in von Kressen's voice. " Perhaps you know then about this file——"

" Containing the details and blue prints of his invention —yes. I know all about it and also that it is in the safest possible hands now, where you and your fellow-scoundrels will never get hold of it," Jack concluded triumphantly. It was something to imagine what von Kressen's crestfallen expression must be if he could only see it at this moment. His voice, after a moment's pause, sounded almost as calm as before, although there was a new note of unmistakable, hardened gravity in it which Jack couldn't miss.

" Indeed! That's a pity. Because if you were able to hand it over to me, it would probably be the means of saving his life."

" Do you mean to tell me that is the condition you spoke about?" Jack asked incredulously.

" Yes. I said you wouldn't like it."

" Like it! Good heavens, it's——" Jack's voice and vocabulary both alike failed him, as he sat staring out into the blackness and listening to the now distant gunfire, while contemplating what seemed to him the most appalling piece of disloyalty and dishonour ever proposed.

" What you're asking is utterly out of the question," he said at last. " You must know that. Even if I'd help to dishonour my cousin in that way, the people who've got the file would never dream of handing it over to you."

" You could try to get it at least."

" And play into your hands—become the same sort of creature as yourself? I tell you I'll have nothing to do with the business. Peter wouldn't want me to—Peter would curse me if he knew I'd consented to do what you asked. He'd tell me to refuse, he'd——"

" Would he? I wonder. Before you say any more, I'd like to show you something which may make you change your mind about your cousin's opinion and wishes."

" I won't—I couldn't——" Jack began, then fell miserably silent as he heard faint rustlings and fumblings in the darkness beside him and waited for von Kressen's next move.

In another instant there was the crackle of paper being

unfolded, then the click of a torch, a faint wavering gleam.

" I don't think a momentary glimmer will matter now —there! Can you read that?"

A blurred dim circle of light shone upon a white surface.

Jack at first could read nothing. He only stared stupidly at the well-shaped hand which held the paper, small, white-skinned and sprinkled with bright copper-red hairs, the same colour as von Kressen's eyelashes.

Then the black lines on the paper took shape as writing, formed letters, words, steadying themselves gradually until Jack could read them quite easily.

" To my cousin, John Frere, or anyone whom it may concern. It is my wish that File 45 should if possible be delivered to the bearer of this note. Peter Loring."

" You recognize the writing?" von Kressen asked softly,

" Yes. It is my cousin's," Jack answered.

" You are convinced, then, as to his wishes in this matter?"

" No, confound you, I'm not!" Jack burst out violently. " I believe that he wrote this only under pressure, that he'd been tortured or something to make him do it—he never would otherwise."

" Then if you think that, it ought to make you all the more careful how you act," von Kressen said gravely. " If the file is not handed over, other means may be taken to get what is required, from Captain Loring. The Gestapo has its own methods—some of them not over gentle, either."

" You're threatening me?"

" Oh, no, not you. It is your cousin who will suffer— unless you do something to prevent it," von Kressen purred softly. " But if I have to go back empty-handed, I can't answer for the consequences. They may be very terrible."

For some minutes Jack sat silent, chilled and horrified by the threatening note in the soft low voice.

" I can't promise anything. It doesn't rest with me," he

said. " But I will ask for the file and tell you the answer, if you fix a place and time."

" This same place, at the same hour in—say—four days' time," von Kressen answered promptly. " And I can only hope that you will be successful. Well, there's the All Clear."

As the long-drawn notes sounded, Jack emerged from the pill-box and went on his way into the darkness. He had made no response to von Kressen's last words. After all, what would be success?

CHAPTER VI

Browned Off

" And that, I think, is where you may have made a slight mistake," Colonel Parker said with a cold, almost contemptuous deliberation, leaning back in his desk chair and looking steadily through Jack with those steel-blades of eyes.

The detachment of his tone made Jack suddenly and perhaps unreasonably angry. It was somehow unbearable that anything of such vital interest to himself should be treated as trivial and unimportant, a slight affair, which didn't really matter much to anybody, least of all to Colonel Parker.

" There's certainly no mistake, sir, so far as I'm concerned," he retorted. " I heard the voice myself on the wireless, and it was my cousin broadcasting. I only wish I could possibly believe I was wrong—I'd give everything I have in the world to be able to think so. But—I can't."

" Try," the colonel advised, in the same cool, impersonal voice as before. " And if you can't manage to convince

yourself, leave it at that. You know your cousin's voice well
—naturally: equally naturally, you are unwilling to credit
even the possibility of his being a traitor of a particularly
vile kind. You must make up your own mind about that;
I cannot offer any opinion. It would be wiser, I fancy, to
assume nothing at all; jumping to conclusions is generally
a mistake."

As he spoke, Colonel Parker's eyes never changed, never
shifted. Jack, staring across that intervening desk, found
them to-day utterly unfathomable, their steel-grey tarnished
and clouded, as it were. They seemed expressionless, almost
soulless, a blank wall, which offered the boy no help or comfort in his desperate perplexity and anxiety.

The rest of the interview had been, up to a point, satis-
factory. Jack had asked for and been granted a day's leave
by his own colonel to go up to London on urgent private
business. Making his way straight to the War Office, he
had found little delay in reaching Room 211X, and to 2nd
Lieutenant Frere's surprise and relief Colonel Parker
nodded grave approval when his promise to von Kressen
in the dark at their interview was divulged.

" You acted quite properly," he said. " You will meet
him at the time and place as arranged and hand over the
file."

With some difficulty Jack camouflaged the gasp of surprise which escaped him. He had quite expected to be
called over the coals, to be told that his action was entirely
undefensible.

And now—here was the colonel unlocking a safe before
his astonished eyes, producing the well-remembered black
file, telling him again to give it to von Kressen and neither
ask any questions or answer them on his own account.

" Keep your mouth shut and your eyes and ears open.
Take very careful notes of anything he tells you as to your

cousin's whereabouts and report it to me, in writing, as nearly word for word as you possibly can," the colonel concluded.

"Yes, sir, I quite understand," Jack said mechanically, but meanwhile his brain was working overtime and coming to certain conclusions which provided an explanation of sorts.

Probably, he reasoned swiftly, the particulars in the file, giving the details of Peter's invention, had already been altered by the War Office experts, so that they would mislead rather than help.

It wasn't in the least likely, so he wisely argued, that anything really valuable or essential, anything of such great use in warfare, would be so calmly handed over on demand to the enemy, even in order to save Peter's life.

He might have done it himself, if it had been in his power, but not the British Government, through the War Office itself. That simply wasn't conceivable.

However, Jack wisely kept all these conjectures to himself, as he took charge of the file of papers and plans which Colonel Parker handed over to him across the desk. He wished now that he had been as discreetly silent on other matters.

But his anxiety was too keen, his fear for Peter's safety made him over-eager for reassurance, when he told the colonel about that note which von Kressen had shown him, in the too-well-remembered handwriting. The older man agreed that it might quite well have been obtained by force, that it did not really prove Loring's own wishes in the matter.

But he made no further comment, which perhaps should have warned Jack that he was on dangerous ground—only he longed so much to hear what Colonel Parker made of the broadcasting mystery, to be given some possible explanation which would confirm his own belief in Peter's innocence.

Perhaps the things which could not be put into a letter, might be said, face to face, by word of mouth; it did not seem too much to expect.

Because he had hoped for this more confidently than he knew, Jack's disappointment was now all the more acute and bitter, as he met Colonel Parker's stone-wall gaze and realized that the interview was at an end.

There was nothing more to be said, nothing more that he could say. He stumbled to his feet rather blindly.

" Is that all then, sir?" he asked. " I mustn't waste any more of your time."

" No," the colonel agreed calmly. " Send on your report of the interview with von Kressen to me as soon as you can and you will be given any further instructions or information."

Descending the War Office stairs, walking afterwards up Whitehall, Jack tried to think over the interview clearly and dispassionately.

Of course, he told himself, Colonel Parker had much more important things to do and consider than this affair. He couldn't be expected to be bothered with that fractional part of the army represented by Jack himself, or even his cousin. It would be foolish to think that he would spend much of his time trying to unravel what must seem to him such a very small and unimportant mystery.

And yet—surely he need not have been quite so callous, so completely indifferent to ordinary human feelings. He hadn't seemed like that the first time Jack saw him, he'd looked kind then; why, even the expression of his eyes had changed.

Hadn't someone called eyes the index of the soul, its windows—or was that just a school copy-book heading

which didn't mean anything in particular? Anyhow, the
colonel's windows had a good black-out covering them up:
you couldn't see any lights, or any soul either. People
talked about speaking eyes, too; in that case, Colonel
Parker's weren't saying anything to give himself away.
Might as well have been dumb for all they told you.

Funny things, eyes, Jack meditated, watching the traffic
and the passing crowds almost unseeingly. Somehow they
seemed to have been playing a big part in his life lately.

Colonel Parker's . . . and those bright-brown, russet-
fringed eyes of von Kressen's, the red lashes half hiding
that glance of sly intrigue, of astuteness and—and—No, it
was hard to describe the expression, but they couldn't be
forgotten or mistaken.

Peter's eyes, looking so tremendously blue and bright
after they'd been ski-ing or skating together, or tramping
across the Surrey hills . . . but it didn't do to think too
much about *them*. Jack switched hurriedly to another pair
of blue eyes, also quite important factors in his life lately.
The O'Morough-Ryan's, changeful, daring, brilliant, light
and dark alternately like the sea when cloud-shadows pass
across it.

" Good lord, I'm getting quite poetical!" Jack grinned
at himself. "And over Shanks's eyes, of all people, the
sulky brute! Well, I turned them black instead of blue
anyway, that's one comfort."

Any others? Oh, yes, Richards' eyes—quite another sort
of brown, rather like raisins in a bun, but pretty shrewd
and understanding all the same. Good old Richards!
How fearfully cut-up he was about Peter. It would have
been nice to have a yarn with him, if he'd known where he
was, and talk things over, with someone who'd be sympathetic.

No use wishing, though. He hadn't the slightest idea of

Richards' whereabouts, he'd got to play a lone hand and unravel this difficult problem all by himself, think of some way to get into touch with Peter and learn the real truth.

He couldn't do that except by reaching Germany, since Peter was there—a fantastic idea, unless he got himself taken prisoner by the Jerries, and that wouldn't help matters much.

Almost unconsciously, Jack had turned left at Westminster Bridge and found himself on the Embankment. As well go that way as any, he decided: he could walk on to Waterloo Station and catch an afternoon train back to Southron Bay.

He crossed the road and stood by the parapet under the plane trees, staring at the river. Old Father Thames—he looked a grey and sullen sort of patriarch to-day under the sky's heavy low clouds, not a very cheerful or inspiring sight when one was feeling absolutely browned-off, anyway. Funny expression that—was it in the army or the Air Force that it started, and what did it actually mean?

It hadn't been used before this war, anyway, and it described a certain state of mind awfully well—the mood when one was fed-up, not so much in the blues as in the browns. Fitted Jack's own feelings just now, especially since brown seemed to be his fated and fatal colour at present, everything surrounded with a kind of halo of brown radiating from von Kressen's sinister russet-clad figure, like a peasoup fog.

And he didn't see any way of getting clear of the browned-off atmosphere—that was the worst part of it.

From a break in the heavy clouds a single arrow-shaft of sunlight shone through, striking the sullen surface of the river, gilding its dun greyness to a sudden glory.

Jack glanced skywards and saw something, already golden, burnished to splendour by the same rays, outlined against that patch of watery blue between the cloud masses.

It was the great gilt eagle of the Royal Air Force War Memorial, poised high on its column as though ready for instant flight, with its wide-spread wings and steadfast gaze turned across the river, away to the sea, the Channel and the far lands beyond.

"Per Ardua ad Astra." Those were the words engraved on the plinth of the memorial—the R.A.F. motto and a grand one too, something to be proud of, something to cheer a fellow up and make him feel that things were worth while, after all.

That other bit too—somewhere in the Bible, wasn't it? —"They shall rise on eagles' wings . . ."

And then, as though in answer to the boy's thoughts, something appeared in that widening blue gulf of sky.

Another glittering bird, wide-winged and marvellously graceful, speeding swiftly across, on into the cloud-continent beyond. Then three close together in perfect formation, wing-tip to wing-tip, followed by another three. From very high and far-away came the sound of engines: Spitfires, on their way across the Channel, flying towards the Continent.

A fine sight, those fighting aircraft—and, by jove, they and the big golden eagle had given Jack a practical idea, too, something almost like a sudden flash of inspiration.

"Why didn't I think of it before?" he thought. "Of course—that's the only road for me to take into Germany, the one way I can get there—by air! Easy enough if I was in the R.A.F. like those fellows, but as it is . . . Paratroops, that's the answer! Just about the only one, as I'm a soldier and not an airman. Join the Special Service troops—volunteer for Commandos. I think they'd take me on all right, as I'm pretty fit and all that sort of thing."

Drawing himself up, Jack clicked his heels together and solemnly saluted the great golden bird, aloof on its pedestal.

" Thanks for giving me the big idea, sir," he said. And swung off along the Embankment, in the direction of Waterloo Station.

He felt a new man, enormously cheered by the very thought of making a fresh departure, of having a real objective to work for, something to get his teeth into, which might lead to clearing up the mystery and saving Peter.

The " browned-off " mood had completely passed, and Jack's one idea now was to get back to Southron Bay as soon as possible, see his colonel and put matters in train.

Jack's new plans worked out even better than he had hoped. The colonel put no obstacles in his way: on the contrary, he was most encouraging.

" We shall be very sorry to lose you, of course, Frere: you'd settled down to regimental work well. All the same, I am sure you're the type they want for the Special Service Troops," he said. " And I don't feel that I ought to do or say anything to prevent you from volunteering. You realize that the training is strenuous—very strenuous?"

" Yes, but I shall like that, sir, although that doesn't mean I want to leave the Royal Westshires."

" Well, you won't really be doing that after all. Because you volunteer for commandos, you don't cease to be a Royal Westshireman, you know. And I quite understand that things have been a bit difficult for you lately, Frere, a bit upsetting. It didn't seem much good to say anything, but I was sorry, very sorry. It's a bad business and I only hope for everybody's sake that it will be cleared up soon."

As Jack left the office, cheered and warmed by Colonel Watson's sympathy, he could not help comparing his attitude with that of Colonel Parker—much to the latter's disadvantage. And he knew much more of the circumstances too, might have been expected to understand all the difficulties better.

" Well, I suppose I was a silly ass to think I mattered a hang to him; I shan't make the same mistake again," Jack decided, and proceeded to compose his application to the powers concerned, to be allowed to volunteer for commandos.

That job completed, there was nothing to be done except wait for an answer and carry on as usual, in the meanwhile. Not quite as usual, though, until that piece of business was concluded which Jack thought of with a mixture of dread, dislike and desire.

He longed to claim the fulfilment of von Kressen's promise and learn Peter's precise whereabouts, but at the same time, hated the necessity of meeting the spy again and handing over the file. It wasn't his doing, he was only obeying orders: all the same, it seemed like giving in to the enemy, betraying his cousin.

The actual interview turned out to be quite unlike Jack's expectations. The night of the appointment was one of misty moonshine, and the boy walked along the esplanade to the rendezvous, carrying the precious file tucked under his arm, concealed by his greatcoat.

The pill-box looked like a pale puff-ball in the dim light and through the black slit of the entrance a faint guiding glimmer showed.

This time Jack took no precautions: perhaps he felt that what he carried would be sufficient protection. Walking straight up to the pill-box, he entered, made out a dark figure and spoke without any other greeting.

" I've come."

" And not empty-handed, I hope," von Kressen's voice said insinuatingly.

" I've got the file, if that's what you mean. I was told to give it to you."

" Good."

" But I'm not going to hand it over, all the same, until

you've told me exactly where Captain Loring is, as you promised."

"I will tell you, although I can't see that the knowledge is likely to be very profitable." Jack saw the other hitch his shoulder forward in that shrugging movement. "Unfortunately, I can't also ask you over to spend a week-end with your cousin. Besides, he might be moved at any time, if our Führer orders it: his abode may have already been changed."

"There's no need for all this talk," Jack broke in impatiently, then caught himself up, remembering Colonel Parker's instructions and added more quietly: "Tell me where he's imprisoned, to the best of your present knowledge."

"Imprisoned is not the word," von Kressen objected. "Captain Loring is an honoured friend and willing guest of the Reich——"

"That scarcely agrees with what you said the other night about the danger he was in from the Gestapo!" Jack burst out.

"So long as he behaves like such a friendly guest," the other finished. "Well, then, my latest information is that Captain Loring has an apartment in Schloss Adlonroth, which, as you may perhaps know, is situated in the Rhineland. The scenery round the castle is most beautiful and romantic: it is also a very safe place near one of the Führer's favourite residences. So that altogether, no guest could desire pleasanter surroundings. And that, I'm afraid, is all I can tell you," von Kressen concluded.

Once again, bearing Colonel Parker's words in mind, Jack refrained from saying that he could have done without any of that guide-book stuff. In grim silence, he handed over the file and von Kressen received it, also without comment, merely bowing stiffly.

"There's nothing more, then," Jack said.

" Nothing more, I thank you," von Kressen answered. " So . . . good-bye till we meet again."

" Which I hope will be never," Jack thought with a considerable lack of prophetic foresight, as he returned to his billets, and sat down to write a full account of the interview for Colonel Parker.

His memory was good: he felt pretty sure that he had not forgotten a single word of the conversation, but it looked pretty poor stuff and entirely uninformative, set down on paper.

Still, there it was: the colonel had told him to report everything exactly, as nearly word for word as possible, and he had done so. Jack, after a few moments' thought, added a brief note, saying that he had volunteered for commandos and hoped very much to be accepted. Then he went out to post the letter, with a sigh of relief.

He had finished that job, anyway. If the next worked out according to plan, Jack thought he would like it a great deal better.

CHAPTER VII

Paratroops

" Talk about leading a double life—anyway, it's life *at* the double, eh, Greg?"

Jack Frere spoke between gasps. Even after a month's intensive toughening, that mile-sprint up and down hill, in full marching kit, ending with a five-hundred yards swim through the cold, wind-roughened river and a scramble up the steep muddy bank on the farther side had left him a trifle breathless.

" Wish I could shake myself like a dog," his companion, Bob Gregory, a lanky Australian, tried to squeeze some of the water from his sodden blouse. " Anyhow, I've managed to keep my Tommy-gun dry, and that's something."

" Come on—another run, in this wind, will soon warm you," Jack told him consolingly, but Gregory groaned.

" *Warm* me, cobber! More likely freeze me stiff. These easterly busters of yours are the iced limit."

The Australian continued his grousing litany as the two fell into step and swung on side by side, up a slope of shaggy heather-covered moorland, toothed with jagged grey rocks.

" That cow of a durned cold bath has started all my skinned patches smarting. Say, had you noticed I'd more and knobbier elbows an' knees than any of the fellows? Must be sort of double-jointed all over and I graze 'em all every time I ' touch down '."

" It's just that you haven't yet got the knack of relaxing when you jump and of drawing up your knees to avoid landing-shock. It takes a bit of getting-into," Jack observed wisely.

" Too true! It does," Gregory drawled. " The bumps I've had—even jumping in harness from that ten-foot platform or the high swing—reminds me of falling out of the old loquat tree in our paddock down-under when I was a kid. What's the next stage in the training?"

" Making jumps through the floor-aperture of a dummy fuselage, on the ground," Jack told him out of his six weeks' longer and wider experience of the daily life of an unfledged paratrooper. " That's just so as to learn to take off quickly and accurately, and they set the speed of the actual jump by using special weights."

" Good-oh! That doesn't sound too bad," Gregory commented. " Mind you, I'm not grousing, whatever it may sound like. It's a bonza life, if this place is way back of beyond, and the climate of your little old island something I can't put into words."

"Perhaps you'd better not try, just at the moment," Jack laughed. "But you're right about this job of ours. It makes a chap feel he's getting somewhere—or will sooner or later. That's what I like about it."

"The sooner the better, as far as I'm concerned," the Australian declared. "I've never liked marking time. Why, I'd take my first umbrella-jump from a troop-carrier at this moment, if I thought it was going to land me somewhere overseas—Germany, by preference."

"My word, so would I!" Jack's eyes shone. "But I'm afraid we'll have to wait a bit longer."

"And, in the meantime, there'll be tea and sausages as soon as we get back to camp," Gregory sighed contentedly, as they topped the crest of a hill, first among the scattered groups, and saw the aforesaid camp below them, filling and overflowing a shallow dish-shaped depression in the vast stretch of moorland.

Not that this was how it would have appeared to a newcomer. The camp buildings, tents, hutments and hangars, were all so skilfully camouflaged, with light and dark greens, bracken-brown, granite-grey and heather-purple paint, in broken patches, that they were practically invisible against the background and surroundings.

In those surroundings, Jack was already beginning to feel more or less at home, after transplantation from the blue sea and sky, the seaside town atmosphere of Southron Bay, to these bleak and solitary uplands, half the year wrapped in wet clouds.

But there was little or no time to think of the weather. If Jack had ever imagined regimental life as a private or with the Royal Westshires was busy, he changed his opinion now. That had been a kind of mass-monotony, the training which fitted men to be soldiers: this was specialized individual work, making each man ready for a big job, something which would need everything he was or had, to carry it through.

The whole atmosphere of the commando training at this camp for airborne troops was charged with that electric sense of preparation, in which not a minute must be wasted. It was accentuated by the resonant ticking of a huge clock, mounted on a pedestal in the middle of the camp, measuring off time by minutes, a reminder that everything must be done " on the tick ". For there were no bugle-calls, no shouting of words of command. Each man was expected to be exactly up to time—the time of the great clock—for lectures, demonstrations, exercises, games, physical training, without any reminder or help whatever from outside. He must be there, ready, alert—and no excuses were allowed.

It must be said that few failed to reach this high standard. There was a great diversity of uniforms and badges—Jack had counted at least fifty different regiments and branches of the service—but all the faces had a certain common stamp, the sense of a common purpose.

Determination, courage, earnestness, whether in work or at the strenuous play which was part of it, those were the qualities most clearly shown. An intention to win, a certainty of winning, but only after putting up a great fight, that seemed the keynote of life here: even the steady tick of the great clock repeated incessantly: " We—must—win. . . . We—must—win."

They weren't just boys, these new comrades of his, Jack thought, glancing sideways at Gregory's lean brown face. He himself was one of the youngest there, and he felt suitably humble and new-boyish as a consequence. Most of them, like the Australian, were in the late twenties or early thirties, tough, hard men, who'd seen life and were well seasoned already.

" It's not our method to train young boys as paratroops,

mere children, not old enough to think or act for themselves
—we leave that to the Nazis," the camp commandant had
said in an address to the new draft on the day of Jack's
arrival. "We—want—men;—that's our slogan, men in every
sense of the word—so don't any of you forget it."

Jack's train of thought was here derailed as he and
Gregory reached the camp outskirts and quickened step
in a race for a shower, a change and tea.

It was only after the much needed meal was over that Jack
realized his own tiredness, and felt glad to think that the
next two hours were his own, to be spent as he pleased, with
no time-checking by the camp-clock.

What should he do with those precious hundred and
twenty minutes? Try to secure one of the few really comfortable chairs and a fairly recent magazine in the rest-
room?—have a snooze on his own camp-bed?—write letters?
—No, Jack decided, it would be a sin to waste what was
going to be the first fine evening for weeks in any such
stuffy ways. He'd go out, a little way up on the moors and
find a dry spot, if he could, to lie down and study his notes
for the map-reading lecture that evening.

The heavy drizzle had stopped before he set out: a soft
breeze was clearing most of the clouds away and shredding
the thin mists which still filled hollows and depressions in
the ground, where shoots of pale-green whortleberries were
showing.

The air felt fresh and sweet this spring evening and smelt
of newly-growing things. The pale-blue sky looked as
though it had been just washed out and hung up to dry.
The wind had shifted from east to south, Jack noticed from
the drift of the clouds: that was why it suddenly felt so
much warmer.

Too warm to walk far: in the first convenient hollow the
boy flung himself down.

" Hot work," he muttered. " Work . . . yes, I must work at those notes . . . in a minute. . . ."

But the minute in question found Jack half asleep and in that drowsy state he remained, not quite sure where he was, uncertain whether certain vague shapes in the mists were rocks, bushes or just figures in a dream, shifting and changing, first one person, then another—Colonel Parker, von Kressen, nobody who could possibly be real.

The last figure who appeared to be there was the least likely of all, but the most solid-seeming. Jack rubbed his eyes. He would certainly have said that he was wide awake now, yet he simply must be dreaming, imagining he saw things.

It was absolutely ridiculous to suppose that the khaki-clad figure, sitting a hundred yards away on the edge of the hollow in a hunched, dejected attitude, back propped against a rock, was really——

" Don't be a silly ass. It can't be!" Jack told himself sternly. " Pinch yourself and you'll know you're still asleep."

Surprisingly, the pinch hurt. Jack sat up, then scrambled to his feet, quite expecting the apparition to disappear or vanish into thin mists. But it didn't: on the contrary, it remained extremely solid, and at the sound of his feet on the dry heather, turned its head.

He opened his lips to speak, but had no time to do more than that before the other got in the first words, spoken with a gasp of amazement.

" Mr. Frere, sir, is it really you?"

" Yes, Richards, it is, though I can't believe my eyes when they tell me I'm seeing you. I thought I was fancying things—I'd been half asleep lying down over there, but anyway, I'm jolly pleased that you're real."

" Well, now, you could have knocked me down with the

lightest feather that ever was, Mr. Frere," Richards was wringing his hand as he spoke, his brown eyes beaming with sheer delight. "You're the last person I'd have hoped to see here and the first I'd have wished for, if you'll excuse me saying so, sir . . . barring one."

No need to say who that was. Jack knew just as well as Richards, and gave the hand he held an extra pressure before letting it fall and motioning to the other to sit down again.

"Let's have a talk and sort matters out," he said. "In the first place, tell me where you've been, and what you've been doing."

"Oh, I just went back to the battery; it's stationed near Colchester. But I couldn't stick it, Mr. Frere—not after I'd heard Captain Loring's voice again, on the wireless."

"Ah, you've listened to it too, then," Jack nodded gravely.

"Yes. . . if it *is* him," Richards spoke wistfully. "When I heard it and—and what he said, I thought the world had turned upside down. But strange things do happen these days."

"They do, indeed, Richards. It's a cock-eyed war, phoney, as the Yanks call it. Yes, I heard Captain Loring's voice all right and, up to the present, I have to believe that it's really him. What do you think of it?"

"Nothing, sir, I just can't; it's quite beyond me. But the Nazis are such arch-fiends, utter devils—I'm sure they're using what the natives in India call *jadoo*—magic." Richards stared at Jack with such owlish solemnity, that the boy could not laugh. "There's nothing else that explains it."

"Sort of hypnotism, eh? Of course, one reads a lot about it and it's practised in many countries, even in England. But if it's that, or whatever it is——"

"Mr. Frere, sir, when I heard the captain's voice again, it was just as though he called me. I—I felt I'd got to get to him—somehow," Richards spoke earnestly. "He's a prisoner over there in Germany, that's certain, and I can't stand knowing that and doing nothing."

"You want to do the good old Blondel stunt, Richards," Jack spoke lightly, but he felt more touched than he cared to own even to himself.

"What's that, sir?" Richards inquired.

"Why, he was a minstrel chap, who was the faithful servant of King Richard Cœur-de-Lion. And after his master was taken prisoner in the wars of the Crusades, Blondel wandered all over Germany and Austria searching for him, singing the King's favourite songs outside all the castles he came across so as to let him know he was there, until he found him at last. . . . Can you sing, Richards?"

"Not much, Mr. Frere, but if I could only get over there I'll whistle myself hoarse, till I make him hear me," Richards said. "That's what made me volunteer for this commando job. It seemed the only chance of getting over to Germany."

"Richards!" Jack jumped up and slapped the gunner on the shoulder. "Great minds think alike, or else it's a clear case of mental telepathy. That's exactly why *I* joined the paratroops too!"

"D'you really mean it, sir?" Richards gasped. "Well, if that isn't another of the miracles of this war! That we should come together like this. Mr. Frere, I think it's just wonderful, and it'll give me a bit of heart to go on, for to tell you the truth, I'd cold feet badly just now. I felt pretty near giving up the whole kaboodle—the very thought of those parachute jumps was getting me down."

"You needn't fret, Richards," Jack said encouragingly. "It isn't nice thinking of it beforehand, but that's really the worst part of it. When you've jumped three or four times from 3000 feet up—that's what we begin at, with the first real jumps from the captive balloon—you somehow stop minding it. That's what I found anyway," Jack concluded.

" I'd like to be able to believe you, sir, and I'm sure I
hope you're right." Richards' tone and expression showed
his complete disbelief in such reassurance. " But I never
did like heights. It always turned me dizzy even to look
down from a top-storey window—s'pose I was a fool ever
to volunteer for this job?" Richards shook his head sadly.

" Don't you believe it." Jack was determined to be persistent in his cheering efforts. " My heart was in my mouth
one minute and down in my boots the next, the first time I
knew I'd got to drop off into space, and even now I don't
exactly look forward to the game, although I've been so
much longer at it than you."

Richards sighed.

" When I looked up at that captive balloon this afternoon,
Mr. Frere, I felt I couldn't do it, even if they shot me as a
deserter," he said, adding honestly, " And I feel pretty
much the same still, in spite of what you've told me."

" Well, I'll let you into a secret," Jack said confidentially.
" I've still got the first jump from a real troop-carrier to
look forward to, and I don't fancy it a bit. So you and I
are both in the same boat, so to speak—or the same aircraft.
And as I'll be doing it first, I shall be able to tell you that it
isn't as bad as we expect."

A faint ray of hope lit the solemnity of Richards' pale
round face. It was plain that this suggestion of collaboration
had definitely cheered him, and he was emboldened to make
a further proposal shyly and hesitantly as Jack prepared to
go back to the camp for his lecture on map-reading.

" Do you think, Mr. Frere, that *they*——" the obvious
emphasis in Richards' voice plainly denoted the greater
powers-that-be, " If you didn't mind, that is, sir—do you
suppose that *they'd*—but p'raps you'd rather I didn't—I
don't want to push in."

" I really can't say till you tell me what you're driving at," Jack laughed.

" Well, it was only—as we're working together as you might say, to find out what's become of our captain and to help him all we can, perhaps I could be your batman—always supposing that you're willing I should, Mr. Frere," Richards finished diffidently.

" There's nothing in the world I should like better, Richards, and I feel sure it can be arranged somehow," Jack assured him sincerely. " So let's shake hands on it."

This was how, after the usual forms and formalities, Gunner Richards of the Royal Regiment of Artillery became attached to the personal staff of 2nd Lieutenant John Drummond Frere.

The arrangement was a good one for both master and servant. Each found immense comfort in the fact that there was someone near at hand who had the same complete confidence as himself in Captain Loring, who could be trusted to believe in his honour and loyalty, however bad things might look. The liking they had always felt for each other soon became a very real friendship, and Jack having told his batman of certain events at Southron Bay was certain of Richards' full sympathy when he arrived at his quarters one evening in a stage of raging irritation.

It had been his turn that afternoon for one of those frequent flights intended to make all the paratroops air-minded and air-bodied. This was a part of the training which Jack thoroughly enjoyed, and Richards glanced in surprise at the boy's flushed and frowning face, as he flung down his kit.

" Anything happened, sir?" he asked.

" Yes. *He* has. I told you a new squadron of fighters was being sent here. I went up with one of the flight lieutenants this afternoon in a two-seater—confound him!" Jack exploded.

Richards waited in silence for further revelations, the while he pressed a pair of battle-dress trousers in a perfect crease.

"You'd never guess who it was—the very last man on earth I ever wanted to see again, with his cursed sneering, superior grin. I'd like to have wiped it off his face as I did before."

"Oh, it was *that* one, was it, Mr. Frere," light dawned upon Richards, as he remembered what Jack had told him concerning the occasion when he first heard his cousin's voice in the German broadcast. "The Irish flying officer you fought with over Captain Loring—him with the queer name?"

"*The* O'Morough-Ryan—Yes!" Jack pronounced the resonant syllables with scorn and disgust. "And I'll fight him again if I have any more of his nonsense, don't make any mistake about it."

"Did he—er—say anything, sir?" Richards asked.

"No, he only *looked*. But that was quite enough, and he'll soon find he can't do it, without hearing from me."

For a few moments Richards remained silent, finishing his job with careful precision. Then he spoke again, respectfully but firmly.

"Begging your pardon, Mr. Frere, and I hope you won't think I'm taking a liberty, but I can't help feeling that it will be a terrible pity if people get to think that you're out to make trouble or pick quarrels with this Mr. Ryan, or whatever he's called. It might get you a bad name with the authorities: they might even send you away from here and then—well, there'd be much less chance of being able to help Captain Loring, you see, sir. That's how I look at it."

"And that's how I ought to look at it too, Richards," Jack assented gravely. "It's the only right and decent way, and you're a good chap to remind me of it."

" Then you're not offended, Mr. Frere?" Richards asked anxiously.

" Offended! I should think not: I'm not quite such a rotter as that. There's only one thing that matters to you and me, over and beyond being decent soldiers and doing our duty and all that—which ought to go without saying. And it would be nothing short of criminal if I did anything to mess up our job. After all, what on earth does it matter what The O'Morough-Ryan thinks of Captain Loring or anyone else?"

" That's the idea!" Richards said heartily. " You stick to that and we'll be all right, sir."

" You needn't be afraid. I'll keep the peace, unless the blighter drives me too far. But I don't know what I should have done without you to keep me from running off the rails, Richards."

CHAPTER VIII

Mid-air

What happened at this training camp for paratroops was rather like a transformation of tadpoles into frogs, a complete change-over from one element to another.

" Or perhaps a bit more on the caterpillar lines, 2nd Lieutenant Frere, debating the point with himself, decided. " After all, a butterfly must feel awfully queer when it crawls out of the chrysalis and takes to the air for the first time. I expect the poor brute's thinking every minute that it's going to stage a terrific crash-landing and break a wing or two."

Hands in pockets, Jack stood staring upwards at the wide open space of blue flecked here and there with tiny white clouds. It was almost as busy with traffic to-day as an aerial Piccadilly Circus, that great sky arena; Jack might have been marooned on some such central city island as Eros of the Circus overlooks from his fountain in peace-time, as he watched the incessantly passing streams of aircraft.

Big and small, they circled, dipped, dived, the whole sky-canopy throbbing with the whirring, buzzing, whining of engines, queer discordant music to which the machines danced wildly, with irregular steps and pirouettes, may-flies, dragon-flies, as if rehearsing a ballet against the azure backcloth, bathed in golden sunlight.

Fascinated, Jack still continued to gaze upwards, in spite of a crick in the neck and aching eyes. To his dazzled sight, the aeroplanes seemed to be swimming round and round now like fish in a huge glass bowl. Gold and silver fish, with glittering scales, or those striped, many-coloured tropical kinds, oddly-shaped, with double-forked tails and upright dorsal fins: he'd seen them in aquariums.

Then, like a whale among all those smaller sky fish, a huge dark shape forged its way through that blue trans-parency, gliding along majestically, ignoring the other inhabitants of the bowl, who seemed to scatter at sight of that black and sombre apparition.

Even although Jack had been expecting its appearance, the size and power of the great Whitley bomber took his breath away, as it planed down—down, until it was no more than a thousand feet above the ground. Still breathlessly he waited for that next scene in the drama which, even after taking part in it several times as an actor, never failed to thrill him as seen from the ground. This occasion, too, had a special interest, for Richards was making his first de-scent from an actual troop-carrier, and Jack realized that he was far more nervous for his batman than he had been on his own account when the moment came for the jump.

Poor Richards! Jack knew exactly how he was feeling,

sitting up there in the bomber, on the edge of the square
hole in the fuselage, legs dangling over space, waiting for
the signal to drop.

It must be nearly time now; the Whitley thundered its
way overhead, towards that definite marked-out area within
which the paratroops must drop according to instructions.

There! Suddenly it was falling through space from the
machine, the first lank, elongated shape, something like a
thinner Egyptian mummy, or even perhaps a bomb or
torpedo—not in the least resembling a live human being.

Even when the parachute opened out, gleaming in the
sunlight like a pearly shell, the man attached still floated
downwards limply, an automaton, a puppet. But Jack's
attention was already diverted from No. 1. The second of
the team had dropped; now, after another split-second
interval No. 3 was descending—Richards.

Jack saw him leave the bomb-hole, watched, with heart
in throat, until he saw the parachute expand automatically
as the long air-slide downwards began. But he no longer
felt nervous, for Richards was behaving with cool expert-
ness, steering the canopy down-wind as he had been taught,
so as to be thrown forward when landing, even while swing-
ing violently from side to side, keeping his feet together,
bending his knees to prepare for the shock of touching-down.

He reached the ground, rebounded elastically, then was
on his feet detaching the parachute harness, running towards
the canister of weapons and other articles of war, sent down
for each ten-man team by a separate parachute, distinguished
like that of the team-leader by being of a different colour.

All the ten were down now, had formed into a line of
attackers and disappeared towards their appointed objective, before another Whitley came roaring along, to deposit
its load of paratroops and vanish in its turn beyond the
skyline, followed by another and yet another.

Not until the exercise was over and the " Stand fast " signalled, had Jack the chance of a word with his batman. It was a changed Richards whom he encountered, a man who seemed to have taken on a fresh lease of life. He had grown leaner, either through the hard training or the open air: his once flabby pale face under the round crash cap was browner and thinner, he looked more active, more alert.

" Well done, Richards!" Jack slapped him on the back. " The instructor says you made a practically faultless descent, the best of all the lot, in fact, although it was a good batch on the whole."

" Didn't feel like it, Mr. Frere, before I started," Richards beamed. " And I thought the brolly was never going to open: it seemed like years instead of seconds, and I could have sworn I'd left all my innards behind me, in the fuselage, when I jumped. Still, I shan't mind the next time nearly as much, that's one comfort. I know the worst now, so to speak."

" I only hope I'll do half as well, this afternoon."

" Oh, you! *You*'re all right, sir—quite an old hand at the game."

" Game. . . . Yes, that's what it has been up to now, more or less. But I don't think it'll be long now before we have a go at the real thing, Richards."

" So I rather gathered, sir," Richards answered soberly. " Well, I shan't be sorry, myself. It'll get us a bit nearer to—you know what."

Jack nodded, his eyes again on the sky. There had been a certain tenseness in the camp atmosphere of late, a kind of feeling that great things were in the air. Without being put into words, it seemed to be understood that those chosen for the present series of practice descents and exercises were, if they passed muster, to take part in something much bigger and sooner rather than later.

"It's not duff, this time—it's pukka gen. We're in for it," a young flying officer had remarked to Jack that morning, meaning that the hints, suggestions and rumours, which were part of normal camp conversation, had something solid and material to support them . . . this time.

The rest of Richards' team passed, one of them limping from a sprained ankle, another with a wrenched knee-cap, but bravely trying to hide these disabilities.

"*They* made rather a mess of things, poor beggars—got too excited to remember all that they'd been told," Richards commented. "Hullo—look at the gliders."

They slid by overhead, in threes and fours, gliders carrying small bodies of troops, graceful and silent, except for the thud-thud of their towing aircrafts' engines. A group of men from the Airborne regiment stood near Jack and Richards, watching these comrades of theirs at their skilful evolutions. Their battle-dress was diversified by the jaunty maroon berets, and the badge of the Grecian hero, Bellerophon, mounting Pegasus, the winged horse.

"Tricky business *that* must have been, Mr. Frere," Richards indicated these mythical figures with a jerk of his thumb. "Worse than our own job, eh?—because I don't suppose Ballyruffian, or whatever they call the chap, had a parachute on board the horse to bale out with."

"No. Can't say his rather scanty battle-dress seems to include that article of equipment," Jack agreed, laughing. "Well, I must be off now to snatch a spot of lunch, or I shall be having that sinking feeling, even worse than you did, when it's time to take the drop."

As a matter of fact, neither Jack's spirits nor his appetite were affected in the least by the prospect of the afternoon's exercises. He felt a thrill of excitement in the thought that if, like Richards, he acquitted himself particularly well, it would be another step towards readiness for the great day.

He was not even depressed by finding, when, after lunch, he and his companions collected outside the hangars, that the blue and gold morning had changed face, to show a ceiling banked with heavy grey clouds, below which the aircraft remaining in the sky flew low, silhouetted in black against the sunless background.

The air, too, tasted damp and saltish, for the wind was driving in from the sea, only five miles away, although invisible from ground-level beyond the humped shoulders of the moor.

The row of ten Whitleys looked like gigantic animals, squatting with uplifted noses, the ground-crews fussing round them. Jack was to be in the fourth flight, and he watched the other teams mount into the bombers, while he pulled the zip-fasteners of his overalls more tightly together, made sure that his Sten carbine, ammunition, knife and other accessories were secure and handy, as he stood waiting.

Between the times when each Whitley loaded up and moved off, roaring into the air after taxi-ing across the tarmac, there was a lull, a marked silence, which seemed a long interval to Jack, although it was only actually a matter of minutes.

His team was lining up now: Jack found himself, as number five almost in the middle of the queue, moving on as though to the tick of their great clock, without a single voice directing them.

Inside the fuselage of the machine they took their places, seated round the square aperture in the centre of the floor, their feet dangling over space. The leader checked them over, looked to the fittings of each man's statichute—the official name for the " umbrellas " of paratroops—then took his own place, as the Whitley's engines revved up and they started on their upward journey.

Glancing down, Jack watched the aerodrome diminishing,

melting into the surroundings, saw its human occupants become antlike, then vanish altogether, some time before the lower strata of cloud drifted together under the machine, blotting out the earth as though a great greyish carpet had been unrolled.

The air was clearing up here; it was a new scene, sky instead of landscape, where one was high enough to take a bird's-eye view, above the cloud mists which filled the hollows of the moors.

The wind had strengthened, blew salter. Here and there little jagged patches of blue showed momentarily, while below the dun-purple tops of the coastal hill-range pushed above the clouds. And away and beyond those bare crests—

> "And what did we see?
> We saw the sea!"

Jack hummed aloud to himself.

There it was, dull leaden grey, sullen, angry-looking, under the leaden sky, the horizon almost completely hidden by low fog-banks. Gregory, sitting beside him, who was gazing in the same direction, spoke in Jack's ear.

"See those machines coming in from the sea?—there, playing pussy in and out of the clouds. What are they, at all? Seven—nine—I've lost count, but it looks like a big push of them."

"Some of our coastal command patrols coming in, most likely," Jack suggested.

"Well, p'raps you're right," the Australian drawled, adding dubiously, "but I don't feel just too sure about them myself, all the same."

Jack glanced at his neighbour with sudden uneasiness. Gregory was noted at the camp for his skill in distinguishing the different types of aircraft, and he seldom made mistakes. The machines had now completely disappeared

again among the clouds and any sounds of distant engines
was drowned by the Whitley's own roar. They must be
nearing the landing-area surely? At any moment the big
bombers might begin to slow down, preparatory to the
paratroop team making their descent.

Instead, there came a little stir of movement inside the
machine, as the wireless operator, with earphones attached
over his head, delivered a message he had received from the
ground station to the pilot in his cockpit. He, in turn,
scribbled something upon the pad strapped to his knee,
which was passed along to the leader of the paratroops.
Word went quickly from man to man in the team.

" Large formations of enemy machines—coming in from
seawards—Exercise off—The pilot's taking us back to the
'drome ".

Gregory's mouth set grimly.

" If he can," he muttered. " Didn't I say those kites
were wrong types?"

Jack nodded. Neither he nor any other man in the team
had moved, but there was a feeling of tension, as though a
length of taut-drawn elastic connected one to the other.

The Whitley banked, turned, began to rise quickly.

" Taking us up higher—good move!" Gregory approved
tersely. " Not so much chance of the Huns getting above
us, or sitting on our tail."

"Couldn't we stay and fight?" Jack spoke under his breath.

" Shouldn't stand a chance. Some of 'em are Focke-
Wulf 190's—tough nuts those new Jerry machines and
heavily armed. *We*'re not. No, cobber, the pilot's acting as
he ought . . . he and the other Whitleys have got their
orders. Hullo! There are some of our own aircraft coming
up! Good-oh! Now we'll see some scrapping."

No German machines could be made out: no doubt they
were hiding among the cloud-layers either above or below.

But, as Gregory had announced, three 4-cannon Spitfires and a couple of Hawker Typhoons had flashed into sight and were diving and nosing about the cloud-edges in search of the enemy, much as hounds try round a cover, seeking a scent.

But the Whitley, flying level now, at her higher altitude, kept on steadily, the chug-chug of her engines unchanged, unhurried.

And then, in a breath-taking fractured second, things began to happen. One after another, like a string of greyhounds on a race-track, nine German aircraft dived out of the clouds, with, close behind them, another trio of Spitfires.

Up from behind came more Huns, so that the sky seemed full of swerving, veering, manœuvring machines, closed in, cut off as they were, by the heavy curtains of mist.

" Me 210's, those last swine!" Gregory cried. " Gosh! I do believe there's one of them going to be sent crashing!"

To Jack excitedly watching, it all still seemed unreal, a scene from a film, rather than something actually happening—the blunt-nosed, square-winged German machine, with its crooked black crosses, spitting bullets viciously at the slimmer, more graceful Spitfire, even while it banked and turned in desperate efforts to get away into the shelter of the clouds.

Streaks of red fire, puffs of smoke, rattle of machine-guns and the heavier bark of cannon, heard even above the roar of the bomber's engines, then suddenly a kind of rending, tearing crash, and the Hun disintegrating, falling to pieces, disappearing in a swirl of black smoke through the torn mists below.

That was only the first of a series of dog-fights, as more and more planes joined in on either side, above, below, from all directions.

Jack remembered how whale-like the Whitley had seemed to him that morning seen from the ground, moving majestically among the lesser fish of the air-aquarium. Again, the same thought returned—only now the other machines were schools of sharks, fighting each other, driven off, returning.

But killer-sharks tackle whales, as well as their brother killers. A big Dornier flashed into sight, sped past, not a hundred yards away, her machine-guns blazing at the short range. Bullets spattered against the bomber's fuselage, something whined past Jack's ear, making him duck involuntarily.

" Why, why, they're attacking *us*!" he gasped, and hearing the surprise in his voice, at having become the target, Gregory gave a half-laugh.

" Too true! What did you expect?" he demanded. " We're the big game the Huns are after. . . . And there's Tail-end Charlie getting to work."

The rear-gunner of the Whitley had opened fire—and effectively. The Dornier dipped and swerved, with one wing partly shot away, then went down—down—out of control, in a swirling spiral.

" Good-oh!" the Australian shouted in his excitement. " Let 'em have it!"

In a moment they had become a kind of storm centre, the German fighters tearing past, trying to get in a burst of fire before being tackled in their turn by the British Spitfires and Typhoons. But the Whitley was vulnerable by her very size, and the attackers too many to be easily beaten off.

A cannon-shot disabled one of the bomber's engines and the machine lost speed and altitude in consequence: wings and fuselage were scarred and perforated by many machine-gun bullets, even before another shattering explosion shook the whole fabric, making her reel, throwing her occupants against each other with the force of the shock.

" I take it we're about done——" Gregory spoke in Jack's ear. " The pilot's giving our man the gen."

Next instant the paratroop leader's voice sounded, steady and calm.

" Men—orders are that you bale-out. We're not far from the 'drome, but the pilot doubts whether he can land the machine safely in its present state. I'll give the signal to drop exactly as usual. . . . Now—get ready—and good luck to all."

A second's pause: then the voice again.

" Number One—ready!"

Jack watched the first man drop, with no more flurry or excitement than if it had been the expected practice. Yet the great aircraft was reeling and staggering, the air thick with oil fumes and the sickening smell of cordite. His own heart-beats seemed to be keeping time with the faltering engine.

" Number Two, ready! . . . Number Three! . . . Number Four!" Gregory dropped with a parting grin. And now it was his own turn.

" Number Four, ready!"

" Feet close together . . . knees bent. . . . Don't look down. . . . You've done it before over and over again. . . . The drop's just the same, whether it's for practice or in earnest. . . ."

" Off!"

He had dropped. The usual feeling of leaving part of himself behind—the usual doubt whether the static-cord would part and break out the canopy. . . . There! He was free—falling, the brolly opening, spreading above him like a great flower.

Clouds below him—he'd be through them in a second. But . . . what was that shadow coming right across his parachute?

A machine was close above him, diving down with a screaming whine. No engine noises now to drown those other sounds, only the beating of blood in his ears, as he realized that this was a German fighter, a Me 210.

A quick shattering burst of machine-gun fire, bullets whizzing all round him, like a swarm of angry bees. Confound it all! The treacherous brute was firing at *him*, as he floated down helpless, spinning slowly round and round.

Any fear Jack might have felt was entirely swallowed up in blind fury, his one desire was to get even with this cowardly assailant, this unspeakable swine!

Again the German dived and fired. This time the parachute's canopy was riddled with bullets, while Jack felt a sharp sting of pain and a trickle of blood, where one of them had slightly grazed his ear. He fumbled for his carbine: perhaps he could get in a shot—no, it wasn't possible, and the Hun was coming at him again, the brute!

Crackle—crackle—spit—spat—it was like bundles of crackers being let off, a vicious, evil sound. There didn't seem a chance of escape—and then came a louder rat-tat-tat of gunfire, another winged shape darting down on to the tail of the German, making the Hun plane jink away sidelong.

Jack had scarcely time to realize that the newcomer was British before the ground surged up towards him in a great wave of green and brown, and he was obliged to concentrate all the senses that remained to him on the need to make a good landing.

He managed it somehow, touched down, stumbled forward, recovered himself, disengaged from the harness, retrieved the parachute, executing all the movements mechanically but with precision. And then his knees gave way unaccountably, and he sank down in a tussock of heather. Was he dead or alive? It took a minute or so to decide that vital point, and when Jack reached the conclusion that he really hadn't passed out, that he wasn't even badly hurt, he lay back and stared upwards, at the duel still going forward in the sky, between his rescuer and his late antagonist.

It was a fierce, flashing, slashing close-quarters combat, between a couple of fine airmen, who seemed as much at one with their machines as first-class riders with their horses. But the British flyer was just that degree the better which decided the result of the fight.

The two aircraft crossed and recrossed, the white streaks from their exhausts patterning the watery, pale-blue sky which now showed overhead. The German seemed trying to disengage, dipping and diving, the Spitfire sped screaming after, its four cannon blazing. And then—a shot went home and the Hun crumpled up.

That was how it appeared, wrecked in the air before it fell, a twisted, crushed handful of metal and machinery, falling out of the sky slowly at first, then faster, flames and smoke encircling it, until it sank out of sight behind a rocky hill.

Jack stumbled to his feet a trifle unsteadily. He saw now that as the team leader had said, he was quite close to the aerodrome from which they had taken off; it was not more than half a mile away from where he stood.

The Spitfire to which he owed his life was circling round at some distance steadily and deliberately over the place where the German machine had crashed: now it turned and flew slowly towards the landing-ground. And, as it flew, Jack saw with a thrill of pride, mixed up with passionate gratitude, that dipping swerve from side to side, with its hint of honest swagger, its joy in a job well done—the Victory Roll of the Royal Air Force.

The pilot of the Spitfire had made a perfect landing and was just climbing out of his machine, when Jack reached the flying-field ten minutes later and ran towards him, breathless and eager.

" I say, I'd got to thank you at once," he paused. " It was absolutely splendid what you did, tackling that Jerry swine —I'd have been riddled with holes like a sieve in another few seconds, just as my brolly was if it hadn't been for you. I'll never forget it—never!"

He broke off, utterly dumbfounded.

The pilot of the Spitfire swung round towards him, a long-limbed, lanky figure, and under his crash-helmet the displaced tuft of tousled red hair above the freckled face and half-closed eyes, showing at the moment a glint of mocking vivid blue-green between the lids, of Flying Officer The O'Morough-Ryan himself.

The Irishman laughed first, so infectiously and whole-heartedly that Jack joined in almost before he realized what was happening.

" And don't you wish you'd got to do the polite to anyone else in the whole world?" Shanks demanded.

" No, I don't." Jack found himself blurting out a truth he had hidden from his inmost self up to now. " I'd *like* to be friends with you better than anything—if we could."

" An' why not, faith?" the airman's eyes were widely open now, darkening visibly to a deep blue-grey. " I'd like it myself."

" Would you really?" Jack's voice sounded half incredulous. " Even if I can't change my mind about my cousin?"

" I'd think very poorly of you if you did!" Shanks declared unexpectedly. " And I want to say I'm sorry for what I said: it was rotten of me, in the circumstances."

" Thanks, I'd like to be able to prove to you that I'm right about Peter Loring, that he isn't a traitor. Perhaps I can—some day."

" I hope so. I'll help you to do it if possible—but you

won't succeed by never listening to him," the Irishman said shrewdly. " You ought to hear what he says. Oh, I know it'll hurt like blazes, but it's a bit cowardly not to try to pick up a clue in that way, don't you think?"

" Perhaps you're right." Jack flushed. " I *have* been a coward about it. I'll listen in future, whenever I can."

" So'll I, and then we'll compare notes. Come along to the mess and have a drink on the strength of it—drink to our own healths."

If the other members of the squadron were surprised to see the pair enter in obvious friendliness, they did not show it; after all, old Shanks was always something of a law unto himself—not the sort of fellow you could criticize, even if you wanted to.

As for Jack, he did not want to. He was entirely content with the fact that his one-time enemy had turned himself right-side-out and become a friend.

CHAPTER IX

Zero Hour

" Have you heard the news, sir?"

" Wha' news?" Jack blinked sleepily at Richards over the rim of his morning mug of tea.

" I had it from Colonel Polton's batman, and he's not a chap who talks without something to say." Richards looked unwontedly flushed and excited, although he spoke hardly above a whisper. Yet he dropped his voice still lower on the next word: " Invasion!"

" By jove!" Jack was out of bed in a minute. " D'you mean that the Jerries have actually landed, that we——"

" No, no, Mr. Frere! It's the other way round—they're going to be invaded by us, at any time now, it seems. Five divisions, they say——"

" By—jove!" Jack repeated unoriginally. " When—where?"

" Any minute!" Richards declared recklessly. " Somewhere in France."

.   .   .   .

" Heard the news?" Gregory asked under his breath, as he slid into the chair beside Jack at breakfast.

" Depends on what you mean?"

" Invasion. Combined operations in big strength at last. U.S. and Dominions, as well as British troops—the Home Guard'll be left to defend the little old island. They say a million paratroops will be employed to do the first part of the job. . . ."

.   .   .   .

That was only the sensational beginning of rumours. They grew even more definite during that day and those which followed, spreading as much by some sort of telepathy as mere word of mouth. Would-be tacticians among the troops discussed plans for the attack in Y.M.C.A. huts and canteens, junior n.c.o.s decided exactly how the operations should be carried out if they were in command of the affair.

Up to this point, the rumours were more or less on the lines of many others which had preceded them. But now things began to happen which gave the whispered campaign an appearance of shape and solidity.

" This business is becoming a bit beyond a joke," Gregory told Jack. " D'you know there are big troop movements going on, towards the coast, whole districts closed to everything except military traffic: and the residents evacuated at a few hours' notice? I'd not mind betting that it's bonza, this time, the real thing—Zero hour."

Jack felt the creeping thrill of excitement down his spine at the words Zero hour—that fateful time at which so many millions of the British army have begun operations, when watches are synchronized and the forces stand on their toes, ready, waiting.

What is known in army parlance as the chain of responsibility was functioning through all its links.

In orderly rooms adjutants pondered over large-scale maps. Quartermasters got ready their last-five-minute boxes, company commanders were busy with platoon commanders holding kit inspections, army transport overhauled innumerable fighting vehicles, while the troops themselves wrote carefully-censored farewell letters home and hugged their rifles with parental affection.

In higher, more distant regions, generals and staff, locked into offices with a red-light danger-signal over the door, denoting " not to be interrupted ", dispatched A.D.C.s with urgent messages to departmental staff officers, buried to the eyebrows in papers and maps, who answered on reams of typed foolscap in that language sacred to themselves and the army.

Telephone-bells tinkled incessantly and impatiently: orderlies rushed hither and thither intoxicated with the consciousness that they, of all the rank and file, were alone in the great secret.

But soon Europe and the world became aware that some big event was pending. It was announced in the incessant roar and throb of aircraft engines high above the narrow seas, over France and the other occupied countries, bombing railways, ports and airfields, marshalling yards and factories, clearing the way for what would surely come.

Then the voices of the B.B.C. took the air, speaking in

almost as many tongues as those at the building of the Tower of Babel.

French and Belgians were warned to keep away from the coast, to stay in their houses, not to try to take part in what was coming and coming soon. But they would not have to remain quiet and inactive long, their chance, too, was near, nearer perhaps than they—or the enemy—expected. The call to action, to battle, might come to them at any hour, broadcast by the Allies to the enslaved countries, above all to those in France who were still free in soul.

" At any hour," the announcer repeated, while German and Italian newspapers snarled back in an uneasy nervousness: " We've heard all that before—we don't believe in your threats—we shall expect invasion when we see it, it has taken place in words so often——"

But the Axis newspapers only reflected dimly the far greater uneasiness of the German High Command, the leaders of the Luftwaffe and the other armed forces of the Reich. For the camera-eyes of their reconnaissance aircraft had seen many preparations which in their opinion obviously meant business of the grimmest kind; the barges and light craft in crowded harbours, camps springing up— signs which could not be hidden from air-spies, like the presence of innumerable newly arrived machines on coastwise airfields.

" Germany calling—Germany calling!" Peter Loring's breathless characteristic voice sneered delicately over the air. " Don't make any mistake, England! We are watching all your preparations—and making our own. You won't take us by surprise."

" That's true enough. I was intruding over France to-day, dropping a few eggs. . . . *I* saw their troop-concentrations. . . . Beg pardon, Mr. Announcer: Over to you, over!"

The voice resumed deliberately, and Jack, listening in

accordance with O'Morough-Ryan's advice, writhed inwardly and longed, as he always did on these occasions, to be a thousand miles away.

" —French coastal areas have become a stronger and better Siegfried line, manned by *soldiers*—not amateur fighters, whose only tactics have apparently been learnt on those world-famed if rather over-rated playing-fields of Eton, where British battle-training traditionally takes place. To attack those iron and concrete ramparts, the English will need some of that Dutch courage which—if history is correct—the early morning rum-ration lent them in the last war."

" Gur-r-r !" growled Shanks, his red hair bristling like that of an affronted Irish terrier. Then, remembering Jack's presence, he caught himself up with a: " Sorry, old fellow !"

But Jack was listening too intently to notice his companion: something which Peter was saying now arrested his attention.

" —And if those French beaches and sand-dunes look safe and innocent to your British air-observers, if you think landing on that coast will be an easy matter, I remember a remark once made to a young relation of mine, that a bird's-eye view isn't much good if there's only a bird's brain behind it, and that even little birds mustn't believe everything they see and hear."

Jack's heart beat fast. Newland's Corner—yes, they'd been there when Peter said that before, in the Easter holidays six or seven years ago. He could see, in memory, the exact place where they sat, his cousin gazing with half-closed eyes at the wide panoramic view.

Was it possible—could Peter be sending a message to him, on the off-chance that he might hear—and understand its meaning?

With a start, the boy realized that the airborne voice had ceased, leaving Shanks free to speak.

"As I was saying when I so rudely interrupted the announcer a few minutes ago, there's a lot of very active military movements going on over in France—thousands of troops being entrained from Germany—heavy stuff too! aircraft flying to the 'dromes round Paris from as far away as Crete and Rhodes *and* in a deuce of a hurry. Oh, our dear friend Jerry's got the wind up, good and proper, about this invasion business. He's not taking any chances."

Jack opened his mouth to speak, then closed it again. No, he couldn't mention that message even to Shanks. After all, it was private, meant for him alone, if anybody, just to tell him not to believe all he heard. Well, he never had, really—but it was an immense comfort and encouragement to have even this shadowy confirmation of that trust in his cousin which seemed so unfounded.

Next day, the tension in the atmosphere had increased: it was known that more troops of the command had been entrained and embussed down to the south coast, that the Canadians from a neighbouring town had disappeared during the night to an unknown destination.

Every hour, every minute, Jack and his comrades in the moorland camp expected their own marching orders. But those orders did not come: instead information reached the air station which sent Shanks striding over in search of Jack, in a white-faced and green-eyed fury.

"We're not wanted!" he cried. "We're going to be left here to hold the baby, while others have the fun!"

It was a crushing disappointment. Watching Shanks pace the floor, letting off steam in a spate of curses, Jack wished he could do the same, not just sit dumbly, feeling like a small boy deprived of a treat, hot-eyed, with a big lump in his throat.

A dense cloud of depression descended upon the whole camp. All their work and training seemed wasted, since, evidently, they were not thought worthy of a share in the real Big Business.

But late that evening a small military car slipped quietly along the moorland track to the camp headquarters. It had only two occupants, the driver and a tall broad-shouldered man in a heavy overcoat.

For hours the newcomer remained in conference with the staff. Then word went round summoning all commandos to the big army hut, where mass lectures and demonstrations were held.

Then the visitor addressed them, standing rigidly erect, hands in the side pockets of his dark-blue jacket, head thrust forward, with only the keen grey eyes under bushy brows showing every movement, as he spoke in short, concise sentences, packed with information of the most startling kind.

He was there to give them certain instructions, the stranger said. They were to be the spearhead of a great thrust at Adolf Hitler himself.

A queer fierce buzz of excitement rose, only checked when the level, rather harsh voice went on speaking.

" You've no doubt heard rumours of serious disaffection in Germany, especially among the Rhine and Ruhr armament centres, bombed by us so incessantly. Those rumours are true. We've absolute proof. So true that Hitler has been compelled to move. He's to address a mass meeting at Drachem and try to dope the workers with talk. That's where we come in."

Again the rising hum, again the steady quelling voice, disregarding interruptions.

" Drachem is close to the Dutch frontier. Nearer still is a large house, Schloss Schwartzigen, which is to be Hitler's headquarters for a couple of days and nights. Our plan is to surround this building with paratroops, taking the guards by surprise, seize Hitler and carry him into Holland."

"For the love of Mike! You'd think he was talking of a sack of potatoes!" Gregory interjected *sotto voce*, but Jack could only ejaculate:

"Gosh! What a man! What an idea! Keep quiet, can't you, Greg!"

"Dutch patriots are co-operating in this scheme," the speaker continued. "They have constructed a secret airfield near the frontier. Here our machines can land to wait for the paratroops. They also undertake to put the German frontier guards out of action, taking their place. This enables our men to reach the rendezvous in Holland—with their prisoner. Also it provides a landing-ground for supporting glider-borne troops, with light tanks.

"The special duties of troops taking part in the raid are allotted. Intensive practice will occupy the next five days. On the sixth day, I shall personally give the final instructions. Zero hour is midnight on the seventh day. That is all, I think."

"All! Jee-hosh-a-phat!" Gregory gasped.

"Who *is* he, anyway?" Jack asked their team leader, as they left the hall.

"Rear-Admiral——"

"You could see he was a N.O.——"

"Major-General——"

"Here, we asked who that particular guy was—not for an army list!" Gregory broke in.

"Air-vice-marshal Sir Michael McGilligan, deputy chief of combined operations," the team leader concluded imperturbably.

"Strewth, he's a blinking combined operation in himself," Gregory remarked irreverently. "But I'd say the man's a leader."

For the five days which followed all interest seemed focused upon a huge sand-table which occupied most of the floor-and-furniture space in the big room, where the training was carried on.

It reproduced down to small details, the terrain round Schloss Schwartzigen, with every road, footpath, irregularity of ground, building, copse and stream indicated. Each paratrooper was provided with a map on which his own precise objective was marked out, and every inch of country was gone over and over again, every action rehearsed in that series of movements which began the instant they touched down which converged upon Hitler's headquarters and must be synchronized to a second.

Models, pictures, photographs, even gramophone records to give sound reproductions of German words of command —all these were used to their fullest capacity.

To the disappointment of both Jack and Richards, it appeared that the latter was not to be in one of these first paratroop teams landed for the immediate purpose of Hitler's capture. He was to share in the raid—that was all he knew, when he was sent to another part of the camp for training, but the two did not meet again before the Whitley bombers went up on the great night.

Sir Michael McGilligan had appeared among them with even less parade than before, the previous evening. He had spoken to each individually, then addressed the whole body of troops.

" You've been picked for an important job: see to it that you're worthy. You know what you've got to do—do it ! But I'll tell you one more thing, now that there's no danger of it leaking out. All those apparent preparations for the invasion of France were a gigantic bluff—to cover this operation of yours, to draw off the Germans. The countless troop-trains moving to the coast—many of them empty. The huts and hangars, the aircraft themselves—just wooden laths and canvas meant to deceive. And they've done the trick.

" There's no bluff about those armoured divisions, those aircraft squadrons which the Hun has moved to France. They're there—waiting for something which isn't going to happen. Not yet, anyway. Well, that's all, I think. . . ."

All! Jack inwardly echoed Gregory's comment. For wasn't it just the beginning, the last directions for the stage manager before the play began?

The world of human folk, of ordinary, furred and feathered birds, seemed fast asleep when they reached the airfield just before midnight, or perhaps only under a spell of silence.

A silver haze, filtering the moonlight through its meshes, gave a complete air of unreality to the scene. It did not even remotely resemble the airfield and its surroundings, seen by everyday sunlight. It was more like the background to some dream where beings from an underworld crept and muttered incantations.

Out in the centre of the flying ground, huge bird-shapes squatted like enormous water-fowl of a prehistoric age, seeming to sway gently as the mists shifted, broke into light and shade.

Yet Jack knew with his ordinary senses that these were only the machines of the fighter escort, ready to take off. Shanks would be there, beside his own 'bus, watching the ground mechanics at work, impatient as a war-dog on a leash to make a start.

Nearer to where he himself stood, only distance and time were both alike distorted and deceptive at this strange hour, were huger, darker shapes, ranged just outside the hangars which had held them. Oddly, their shadows on the moonlight-silvered ground seemed more substantial than themselves.

Perhaps that was what happened at these times—shadows

became real and real things shadows. Perhaps those mutterings and whisperings were the shadows of voices, become grotesque like everything else.

Lights flickered here and there, like fireflies or glow-worms—what was that line of a verse about: " the elves also, whose little eyes glow?" " Night-piece " wasn't the poem called?—and jolly appropriate too.

The figures behind the lights looked rather goblinish, demoniacal, bulgy and shapeless.

" No more queer than I do myself, though," thought Jack, glancing down at his bulky overalls, his big fleece-lined, heavy-soled boots, then at Gregory close beside him, similarily attired, surmounted by a crash-helmet—and murmuring something incoherent.

" Hey, Greg, what are you muttering about?" he asked, his own whisper sounding loud as a shout to him.

" Only a thing my mother taught me as a kid down-under. She's a west country woman as superstitious as they make 'em. Made me say it at night—a Cornish litany she called it," Gregory answered somewhat sheepishly. " How did it go?—' From Witches and Warlocks and long-legged Buzzards, and creeping Beasts that move in hedge-bottoms, and things that go bump in the night—Good Lord, deliver us!' "

" Funny—I was thinking about the same sort of thing," Jack said. " But it's about time we chucked it and woke up to work. This isn't a dream—whatever it feels like."

" More of a nightmare—Hullo, the fighters are off!"

The antlike figures were more busily occupied than before round the big bird shapes: they moved to and fro, as though giving a preliminary push and send-off to a swing. The engines roared out: the graceful shapes rose one by one into the air, circled the aerodrome, disappeared.

Then, in a louder, deeper crescendo, the mechanics

started up the engines of the Whitleys. The teams took their places, and the huge aircraft left the ground and followed their escort up into the mysterious night sky.

Once they were air-borne, and he had taken his usual place beside Gregory in the fuselage of the bomber, life seemed to click back into the ordinary normal routine for Jack, the feeling of unreality gone. Excitement and co-operation took its place, as the team discussed their actions of the immediate future.

Occasionally a scrap of information was passed on by members of the bomber's crew.

" We're over the Channel now. . . . Above the Frisian Islands and the Dutch coast. Crossing Holland—that's the River Scheldt: you can just catch the gleam of it under the moon. . . ."

Not far off now, then.

Hands adjusted crash-helmets, fingered weapons, patted pockets and equipment—all those little preparations for a journey's end which travellers make when they hear the name of the last station before their destination is reached.

"Wonder if we shall get much flak," Gregory speculated. " It's very quiet so far."

" I shouldn't think we'd run into a lot at this altitude," Jack answered. " And no searchlights seem to have spotted us as yet. Shanks told me they'd all got orders to keep as high as possible, both bombers and fighters, and not take any chances in that way—keep high until just before we're to bale out."

" And anyway we're not likely to get much night-fighter opposition," Gregory chuckled. " *They*'re being kept busy in France, waiting for the invasion that isn't going to come off—and before they realize *that* we'll be home again—with little Adolf !"

" It would be different if we were trying to land near a

big town with heavy ack-ack defences," Jack said. " As it is, *the* great idea is to try to take them by surprise."

" Ready, men!" came the warning voice of the team leader, and they could feel that the bomber was descending now in a long level glide, not steeply as a lighter machine would.

When they reached the lowest point of that glide, the moment of the paratroopers would come.

" Now!" That was the preliminary signal. " No. 1—ready! Two—three—four—five——"

A moment later, Jack found himself floating down, slowly, his canopy curved above him, white as the little clouds scattered higher still.

Below and above him he could see the parachutes of his comrades, like pearly soap-bubbles, gleaming faintly in the moonshine.

Below again stretched a wide, dim countryside, growing gradually plainer as he descended, grey-white roads, dark patches of woodland, pale fields—the gleam of water where a wide river ran—Germany.

CHAPTER X

Heil Hitler!

Germany—but there was no time to think of all that the word meant, except to realize that this was the real thing at last, what they'd been training for, sweating for—and that he mustn't forget the smallest thing he'd been taught in the preparation for this moment.

Knees flexed, muscles relaxed—but even so, it seemed to Jack that the soil of the German Fatherland, when he touched down upon it at last, was noticeably harder than that of Mother England.

The thought only flashed through his mind, as he detached himself from the parachute, before rolling over and executing that rapid series of cartwheels, intended to steady the nerves and slacken the limbs of paratroops before getting down to their job.

A matter of seconds only, these exercises; then Jack was racing towards the coloured parachute which had brought down the weapon canister, Gregory close at his heels.

" Cursed bad landing I made," the Australian grumbled. " Nearly broke my ankle."

" Can you carry on?" Jack asked.

" Can I? Look here, d'you want to make yourself unpopular? *Can* I? What d'you take me for?"

All was going according to plan. Three men with a Bren gun were already off and away, just vanishing silently into the dark fringes of a wood. The team leader, filling his pockets with hand-grenades, spoke to the others as they bent over the weapon container, taking what was needed. " You all know your job—good luck!"

He was off, a second man close beside him. A few hundred yards away, another team of paratroopers were just descending from the sky.

" That should be the finish of the twelve Whitley-loads," Gregory commented softly, as he and Jack made for cover. " Quite a dinkum push of Hitler-snatchers, but you bet he's strongly guarded. Little Adolf doesn't take risks— so long as he knows where they're coming from."

The last great aircraft showed dark against the silvery sky, and as the sound of its engines died away, an intense silence fell, a stillness which must not be broken by a whisper, a sign, a cough from the intruders on to enemy soil.

It might appear that no living waking man could be within miles of this seemingly lonely spot, yet Jack felt as though the whole German countryside held its breath to hear, strained vigilant eyes to see the slightest movement.

At this very moment a Hun sentry might be standing only a few yards away . . . that faint rustling might be man-caused, not some small creature, a rabbit, or weasel, stealing through the dry grass.

A night-bird cried suddenly, wing-flapping from one branch to another: a glimpse of himself, Gregory, or someone else had frightened it.

The pair were wriggling along on their stomachs now, through a belt of trees and shrubs. These had been represented on the sand-table by twigs and scraps of green-dyed loofah, but the two paratroopers knew, pretty exactly, the width of the strip, and were not surprised by finding themselves close to that ornamental wooden fencing which bounded the estate.

Edging his way up to it noiselessly, Gregory close beside him, Jack raised himself to peer over the palisade and see the original of the snapshots and plans they had been shown of the house they were approaching, which was surprisingly like those pictures.

The name Schloss Schwartzigen didn't mean that it would have been called a castle in England. This large mansion, set in its own grounds, was an ultra-modern edifice, all concrete cubes and blocks, such as the Germany of to-day admires most, like something built by an ogre's child.

Square, flat-roofed, all the framework which would once have been wood replaced by metal, it looked quite out of place among the pine-woods which surrounded it on every side, a mechanized robot of a house in a Grimm's fairy-tale setting.

Built for himself by a wealthy Jewish financier, who had fled from Germany when Hitler came into power, the place had been taken over some time before by the Nazi government and was now used, as the British Intelligence knew, to house their opposite numbers of the Reich secret service, moved from Berlin for safety to this remote country district.

There it stood, pale, expressionless, staring across its grounds with blacked-out, vacant window eyes. No sign of alertness or awareness so far about the building, although it wasn't likely that there were not an adequate number of sentries posted somewhere among the shrubs and gravel paths of the garden.

It seemed almost impossible to realize that the attacking force, a hundred and twenty strong, had surrounded its objective, that those who composed it were already moving forward to their appointed places in small packets and groups.

Yet Jack knew it was so. After such repeated rehearsals he could visualize everything, see in imagination just what points his comrades had reached in their progress.

Like clockwork they'd all be moving, the actual attackers, among whom were Jack and Gregory, well in advance, small squads protecting the flanks, keeping up communication, with those in reserve held in hand within the wood by the commanding officer of the whole raiding force.

All set—even now the scattered lines were creeping on stealthily, inexorably, catlike, panther-like, tiger-like. Knowing each man, Jack pictured them plainly, on tiptoe for the moment when the house itself must be rushed, like runners waiting on the line, taking a last deep breath before the word " *Go*!" or the starter's pistol-shot, alive, alert in every muscle, nerve and sinew.

All set—hidden from each other, yet aware of the presence of every unit of the commandos, in contact with that leader who, like the centre of a capstan, controlled the movements of all its parts, its converging, revolving points.

And, so far, these movements had been entirely un-molested, apparently entirely unnoticed. It was almost beyond belief, yet by some miracle of luck the defenders seemed oblivious to any possible danger.

"You'd think they were asleep or blind," Jack muttered to his companion.

"No, not asleep—and if they're blind, it's blind drunk," Gregory retorted grimly. "There's one real row going on inside the house. Listen!—what good company dear Adolf must be!"

From the house came muffled sounds, and for a second Jack half feared that some of their men approaching from the back might have possibly broken in prematurely, be fighting for their lives, unsupported.

But these weren't sounds of conflict, or quarrelling. Muffled by distance and closed doors and windows came music, the roar of voices singing in chorus.

"That's their beastly *Horst Wessel* song—the Nazi national anthem. I've heard it on the wireless," the Australian whispered.

"S-sh. Look." Jack's voice dropped to the merest breath.

For suddenly into a circular open space of gravel, not a hundred yards away, where four paths met, between hedges of laurel, two figures emerged, stood facing each other.

Simultaneously, their right arms were stiffly thrust up, with the hoarse-barked salute: "Heil Hitler!"

In the dimmed moonlight their uniform of S.S. troops, Hitler's own picked bodyguard, could be easily distinguished, their profiles set and wooden under the steel helmets.

For a moment the sentries stood, while a sharp succession of questions and answers passed: then they saluted again, and went on, tramping along the paths in opposite directions.

"You take that one," Gregory jerked his head to the right. "I'll tackle the other. Time we cleared the way to the house."

Instantaneously, without another word exchanged, the pair were over the fence, moving noiselessly in the shade of the laurel hedge, separately now.

Jack, sprinting on tiptoe, could hear the footfalls of the German he followed growing plainer. The path twisted, and he saw the soldier's square shoulders just in front of him, was upon them in one leap, jamming down the steel helmet with a single blow, before the S.S. man had time to realize what was happening.

He gave one smothered snort, then plunged forward, with Jack on the top of him, and lay, face downward, stunned and motionless. No fear that he'd give the warning now: next second Jack was on his feet again, running, stooping as he ran towards the house, to be joined, before he reached it, by the panting Gregory.

" A bit of a struggle, but I put him out of action—without noise either," the Australian gasped. " How about yours?"

" Outed too—we've been lucky, Greg. There hasn't been any alarm yet. Look, the rest of the chaps are here!"

They might have been a gathering of ghosts converging upon the house, those noiselessly-moving figures, shadows materializing from the shades.

Scarcely a word or whisper passed as the commander made for the doors and windows, silent stormers of the enemy's stronghold.

Meanwhile from within still came the sounds of music, low guffaws of laughter, singing, and a thumped piano accompaniment, loud voices raised in ragged and raucous disunion.

" *Deutschland—Deutschland über Alles*!" they roared, until the chorus was unmelodiously interrupted by a single wavering voice chanting uncertainly the old student's song, " Gaudeamus Igitur ".

It was not surprising that this gathering had not heard

the approach of the raiders: the noise they were making would even have drowned the warning throb and thud of the Whitley bombers' engines.

By this time twenty or more men had joined Jack and Gregory before the main door, among them Captain Borton, the leader of this party of the special service troops. He gave the wailing hoot of an owl, and this was answered from the rear of the house, where a similar unit stood ready at the back entrance.

That owl hunting-cry was the pre-arranged signal for a simultaneous assault, a leap forward by every man. The door was flung open, they hurled themselves in, living missiles, filled with fierce, destructive energy.

The first onrush took completely by surprise and bore down any resistance from the Black Guardsmen near the entrance. Before they could recover themselves one of the commandos' Bren guns had been mounted in the doorway, and its fire power was smothering that from the German automatics, clearing the spacious hall of its defenders.

They retreated hastily into doorways. The air was filled with the spatter of bullets, the crashing explosions of grenades, while flashes of blue, green and yellow flame were reflected from the glass and chromium panelled walls.

The noise in this restricted space was terrific. But Gregory shouted exultantly to Jack as they charged abreast through a side door.

"Too true, it's good to make a row again after all that hush-hush business! Ya-ee-ow! Up the gumsuckers!"

The terrific yell with which he ended, culminated in the crash of another grenade.

The entrance hall was clear now, the raiders, in twos and threes, mopping up the Germans in the adjacent rooms and corridors according to plan. From all over the house came the sounds of conflict, shouts, the cries and groans of wounded men, shots, the rat-tat-tat-tat of machine-guns, solitary reports from concealed snipers, the whine of bullets up and down the scale.

Only the male voice chorus had ceased, with its musical accompaniment, replaced by a confused babble of loud, angry voices coming from the same direction, along a wide corridor which branched off to the right from the hall.

The British leader spoke, indicating this direction to the men whom a whistle had summoned round him.

" That's where *he* is. Come on, and smoke out the wasp's nest! There are men posted outside to prevent anyone escaping through the windows. We've got him trapped!"

"Huroosh! Ya-ee-ow! Hurrah!" A strange medley of triumphant yells greeted the words.

Trapped! The leader of German war-lust, blood-lust—commander of all the evil unloosed to destroy Europe and the world—" that *Bad Man*!" Those two short words seemed to Jack to sum up all the vileness and cruelty against which they were fighting.

He shouted with the rest, as they all went surging forward along the corridor, towards the gleaming chromium-plated double doors which made it a blind alley. It was as though the devil himself was lurking, waiting to be captured behind those closed doors, cornered by mankind at last.

The few German soldiers remaining in this part of the house had retreated hastily towards the big doors and were formed up as though to defend them. But they looked uncertain, glancing, grey-faced, from side to side, seeming to need guidance to force them to make a stand. A few shots and flung grenades from the raiders sent most of the survivors scrambling to take refuge in other rooms opening on the corridor.

" Clear the way, men—clear the way!" the leader shouted. " Break down those doors—quick!"

Six men aside seized a heavy oak bench and swung it forward between them, using it as a battering ram.

Crash! and again Crash! It smashed into the panels, splintering and cracking them, tearing the door from its hinges, sending it crashing inwards over the furniture which had been hastily piled against it, in a ramshackle barricade, over which the men of the commandos scrambled into the room beyond.

Held up himself for a few seconds by the onrush, Jack was able to get a glimpse of that room's interior, over the shoulders of the man nearest him. It was a strange sight.

Near the glowing tiled and metal stove at the far end of the room, stood the long dining-table, and enough could be seen to show that, a little while before, it would have been quite true to say that it groaned under the weight of good things.

Bottles of champagne and wine, dishes of fruit and pastry, boxes of cigars—all these had loaded it. Now, the cloth having been partly dragged off they lay scattered on the ground, among broken glass and china, pools of spilt wine and melting ice puddings.

Behind the table stood, or crouched, a group of men: others sprawled across it, one or two lay huddled on the ground, while more had taken up their stand behind a grand piano, with its lid raised. It was a scene of the wildest confusion, the strangeness of it all increased by the elaborate theatrical-looking uniforms, the glaring ribbons and medals which most of the men wore. Their swords and other equipment hung on pegs or over pictures on the wall behind them.

One figure was particularly resplendent, bulging in a tunic of pale-blue and silver, the broad chest of which was so beplastered with decorations that it looked like that of a tailor's dummy.

He sat slouched in a chair, like an Eastern nabob on his throne, big and bulky, his vast jowl and almost clean-shaved head crimson, but his bloodshot, blue eyes staring stupidly at the intruders, as though he could not imagine who they were, or where they had come from.

Close behind him, leaning on the chair's back, was a leaner, younger man, in a black and brown uniform, who might have been handsome, but for black eyes, set too near together and a thin-lipped sneering mouth. He was obviously less drunk than most of his companions, and his face twisted and writhed in fury and hatred as he fingered a revolver.

Before he could use it, the voice of Captain Borton rang out, clear and distinct.

" Put up your hands! If you don't surrender, everyone of you, we've Bren guns here!"

Even in their half-sodden state, most of the German officers who remained conscious at all evidently understood this very plain English. As for the Bren guns, there were three, in full view, to speak for themselves, as were the grenades which the raiders held ready.

A dozen pairs of arms were thrust up, even before Borton finished speaking, but the big man still slouched and stared, while the other behind him snarled and half raised his weapon again.

" You hear what I said!" Borton shouted. " I'll give you till I've counted ten;—one—two—three—four——"

" Kamerad! Kamerad!" several thick voices shouted desperately, and one fat, pasty-faced colonel clutched at the big man's arm, perspiration pouring down his cheeks.

" My God, Herr General, surrender!" he gasped. " What else can we do? These devils—they'll slaughter us—surrender, and tell the major here to do the same!"

" What? What?" Herr General von Bockenburg stared round stupidly. Then his loose mouth stretched in a wide grin. "Why—why—certainly . . . to oblige you, Herr Colonel—can't do anything else—as you say."

"Don't do it—don't do it, Herr General—let us die rather!" the dark man behind his chair burst out fiercely. "What will the Führer say if we surrender like frightened calves?"

"The Führer—the Führer——" the general mumbled thickly. "Well, Major Dussel, he can't say anything, can he, as he isn't here?"

"*Als Er nicht herein ist . . .*" Jack repeated the German words, then translated them aloud: "He isn't here! Did you hear what the general said, sir? Hitler isn't here!"

"What?" Captain Borton glanced round. "No, by jove, he's not either! Couldn't mistake *him*."

The news spread from man to man. Already, like their leader, they had realized that there was nobody present who in the least resembled the countless pictures of Hitler which they had all seen.

A few curt orders sent off a dozen men to search the house again. Captain Borton strode forward, revolver in hand, and addressed the group behind the table sternly.

"Gentlemen—and especially you, Herr General—I must ask you to tell me at once where Herr Hitler is. We know he's here—we've had positive information on that point. It will only be the worse for you—and him, if you try any tricks."

The Germans stared blankly. Captain Borton burst out with impatience.

"Here, Frere, you speak German—translate for me."

Jack obeyed. His hearers glanced at each other with mixed uneasiness, fear and bewilderment. Only a few showed anger, and Major Dussel growled out aggressively in German:

"You need not suppose that we shall tell you anything—proceed and do your worst——"

But General von Bockenburg was far too drunk to adopt any such heroic attitude.

" Come, come, Dussel," he expostulated. " No good to talk like that—asking for trouble. Why shouldn't they know the Führer's not here—put off coming at the last minute, said he felt it wasn't well, and telephoned he was sleeping elsewhere."

" Be silent, sir!" Dussel hissed, shaking his superior officer's arm unceremoniously.

" I won't—and you forget yourself, Dussel," the general drew himself up with an assumption of dignity. " You know very well dinner was on the table—if it wasn't the Führer, I'd call it most inconsiderate. Not but what we've enjoyed ourselves. *He* doesn't approve of drinking—we couldn't have been so gay with *Him* here."

Jack finished his rough translation of the speech, and Captain Borton burst out laughing in spite of his chagrin.

" I've not the slightest doubt that he's speaking the truth—drunkards do, they say. He'll probably want to blow his brains out when he realizes what he said, after he's sober."

" That's right, sir," Jack agreed. " I'm afraid there's no doubt Hitler funked coming here at the last minute. It's—frightfully disappointing, sir."

" It is—but we've got to make the best of it. Not a bad best either, men, this bunch of important prisoners, including at least a dozen staff officers. Gentlemen, I'm sorry to interrupt what I'm sure was an extremely enjoyable banquet, but I must ask you to accompany us as prisoners of war. Will you give the necessary orders, Herr General?"

The general hauled himself to his feet and surrendered with clumsy attempts at dignity. Most of the others behaved in the same manner, although there were venomous and vindictive scowls from the more sober prisoners, and Major

Dussel spat and muttered curses like a snared wild cat when his revolver was taken from him, seeming almost prepared to resist. His evil mood was not soothed by General von Bockenburg's attempts at consolation.

" Come, come, Major," he said reproachfully. " Do not be so upset. Any one might think you were sorry, not glad, that our beloved Führer escaped capture so narrowly."

But from Major Dussel's expression it seemed fairly plain that he considered his own capture, or something which he represented, of more vital importance even than the fact that the leader himself had not been included in the prizes taken by the British. And light was soon to be thrown upon the reasons for his fury.

CHAPTER XI

"Help!"

The final rounding-up of the prisoners was not a long job. The surviving Germans in the house were already secured, and those wounded had received rough-and-ready first-aid treatment.

They stood about the hall in sulky and despondent little groups, shepherded by their captors, mostly resigned to their fate, although some of the officers were still blustering and aggressive, loudly demanding to be allowed to collect personal possessions, complaining in guttural German of the way in which they were being hustled and hurried by the cursed British.

" They don't seem able even to swear in anything under twelve syllables," Gregory said. " And although I don't know the lingo, most of their talk is bad language, by the sound of it."

The Australian's comments were muffled by the fact that he was endeavouring to tighten with his teeth the knots in a handkerchief bandage round his right wrist, until Jack took over the task.

" Here, let's help. You've a nasty cut there."

" It's nothing—but, my Colonial! I wouldn't mind losing the arm if we hadn't lost Adolf!"

" It's sickening," Jack spoke dejectedly. Now that the excitement of fighting was over, most of the raiding troops felt disappointingly flat, even though they had in many ways been successful, and were likely to find plenty of thrills and danger during their return to the rendezvous.

But on commando there is no time for brooding. Captain Borton's voice broke in on the conversation.

" Where's Major Dussel? I've just heard from one of the other prisoners that he is a most important catch—*the* Big Noise in the Hun Secret Service crowd parked here. Who had charge of him?"

" I had, sir!" a sergeant answered. " But he must have slipped away while I was attending to this wounded chap. I'd not turned my back half a minute though and he seemed to have quieted down."

" Find him!" Captain Borton ordered briefly, and Jack and Gregory, taking it on themselves, were away in a second.

Tommy guns ready, knives loosened in the sheaths, the pair raced back along the corridor to the banqueting hall. Not a sign of life there—except a mouse nibbling the scattered fruit upon the floor, only to scuttle off at sight of the strangers.

Room after room they entered, all empty. Then Gregory, who was ahead, gave a shout, swerving off sideways.

" Here he is! Oh—no, you don't! Drop that, will you— give it up!"

The Australian had disappeared through a doorway and

his voice came in breathless snatches. Jack followed at top speed into a small room, fitted as an office, where Gregory was struggling with Dussel, the two men wrestling together so fiercely that it was hard to distinguish one from the other, as they heaved and twisted, ducked and struck.

"Papers—trying to destroy them," Gregory gasped. "Just going to eat that slip—get it away!"   Frontispiece

Jack joined in the tussle, managing to wrench open the German's fingers, secure the slip of paper, and thrust it into his own pocket. But Gregory, handicapped by his injured wrist, could not hold the desperately struggling man for long. Dussel broke away, snatched up a heavy metal paper-weight from the large desk over which masses of documents were scattered, singly or in bundles, and flung it at the Australian. Fortunately, he ducked just in time to receive it on the shoulder instead of the head, but it served to keep him momentarily out of action and left Jack to tackle the German alone.

"Fetch help!" he shouted to Gregory, as he closed again, and while butting Dussel with his head, kicking his shins, trying to trip him up, he heard the thud-thud of the other man's retreating footsteps at a run.

After that, Jack was too fully occupied for a time to be aware of outside happenings. The German major was strong, wiry and determined and, although unarmed, this fact, in the circumstances, made little difference.

For Jack knew that if it was in any way possible he must secure this prisoner alive, must not use his own weapons to save his own skin. Dussel might be a most valuable source of information—and so the young man fought on doggedly, not only to keep the German from escaping, but to foil his obvious intention of destroying the scattered papers at any cost.

Jack succeeded in hitching his leg round that of his

antagonist, bringing him to the ground. They rolled over and over, wrestling, striking: Jack's head was finally bumped upon the floor, so that he lay dazed and half stunned.

This was Dussel's opportunity, and he struggled to his feet with an ejaculation of triumph and an ugly laugh.

" Take that, you English swine," he growled, and before turning his attention to the documents, kicked out at Jack viciously. That extra touch of brutality was his undoing. Jack had regained his wits sufficiently to make a clutch at the German's ankle. He clung to it desperately with both hands, impeding the other's movements, just long enough to allow help to arrive.

There was again the sound of running feet, Gregory's shout: " Here they are !"—Borton's answering voice. Next instant, two hefty special service soldiers had Dussel by the arms, while he fought and struggled, making it no easy matter to hold him.

" He's telling us pretty plainly how extremely important those documents are, since he's so mad keen to destroy them," Captain Borton commented grimly. " You're not badly hurt, Frere, I hope ?"

" No, sir—only a bit battered and shop-soiled, so to speak," Jack answered. " Here's another scrap of paper we took from him, before he could dispose of it."

" H'm, evidently a cipher code," the leader examined it. " We'll put all this stuff together and send it on to our Intelligence. I've an idea that this haul is something uncommonly worth having."

" He'd got them all hidden away in this cupboard behind the panelling," Gregory pointed out. " Look, sir. We'd never have known it was there if the Hun hadn't slipped off to open it himself: it's pretty cleverly concealed."

" A very smart bit of work indeed, on the part of Frere and yourself. And now the sooner we're off the better, to reach the rendezvous in time, prisoners and all. Just make them understand—especially our dear friend Major Dussel —that we can't allow any shooting, or trying to give the alarm, so they may as well come quietly and not make trouble."

Almost as silently as they had approached Schloss Schwartzigen, the British raiding party left the house. Not a word was spoken aloud: only an occasional whispered order passed from man to man.

Under the guidance of a Dutch refugee, who had accompanied the expedition from England and knew from childhood every track and footpath on both sides of the border, they made direct for the rendezvous at a steady jog-trot. The place was some five miles away, close to the German-Dutch frontier: there a supporting force of British and Dutch loyalists would meet and escort them across that frontier.

The party in reserve had joined the attacking force for mopping-up operations in the house. It would be time enough to scatter, if they met with any opposition and make for the meeting-place singly, or in small groups. So far they had been unmolested, and Captain Borton could congratulate himself on the comparative fewness of his casualties— far less than he had expected from such a desperate and dangerous operation.

The way led throughout that strange black-and-white borderland country, like an etching, with its dark fir-trees and pale sand-hills. The footfalls of the party were deadened on the narrow pine-needle-padded track, and the silence, the soft, regular pace had a sort of somnolent effect on the senses.

Jack found himself almost sleeping upon his feet, as he tip-toed on—on—head sagging forward, eyes half closed. He was well in rear of the small column even at the start, and had lagged behind still more, although automatically keeping up a good speed.

So it happened that there was no one very near him when he first heard the strange sound.

At first, in his state of semi-drowsiness, Jack thought that it was only a night bird, and paid little attention. Then something queer in the sound caught his ear and he halted, listening intently.

Yes—he was almost sure that it was a human voice. There it was again—and this time it certainly sounded like: " Help! Help!"

Jack glanced round. A good many yards already separated him from the rest of the force; even as he looked, the rearmost man disappeared round a bend in the track, and the young officer was left practically alone.

He knew quite well—or at least one part of his mind did —that it was his plain duty to disregard this, or any other appeal, to keep straight on. But something else, some instinct urged him to find out what had happened, to answer the call, and that instinct was strong enough to send him hastening back, almost before he knew what he was doing.

" Help—help!" But was that really the word, as he had taken for granted? " Helfe! Helfe!" sounded much the same—only then it would be in German instead of English, and he might even be running straight into a cleverly-set trap. Jack stopped short in momentary panic. What a fool he was probably making of himself, yet he could not leave the call unanswered.

Mad as it might be, he must keep on, go back and see for himself.

What direction had the voice come from? Over there, he thought, although it was extraordinarily hard to say, with his heart beating with such hard thumps and his nerves on edge, taut with the strain.

Had someone been left behind at the Schloss, or dropped out as they hurried along, perhaps an injured man who had managed to conceal his wound? If so, he might be lying in the undergrowth near the path, not daring to shout again.

Jack slackened his pace and went along more cautiously and watchfully, searching on both sides of the way. There had been no more cries for a while to give him guidance: when a hail came suddenly again, it sounded startlingly near, although weak and hoarse.

Away there on the left—there was no path, so Jack plunged through the sand and twisted tree-roots, more or less blindly, nosing like a fox-hound. The moon had set, and it was very dark, that extra darkness which comes immediately before the dawn.

There was another sound now, growing clearer and louder, that of running water. Jack remembered that a fair-sized river, one of the Rhine's tributaries, flowed within a mile or so of Schloss Schwartzigen: it had been marked on their maps as an obstacle to avoid.

The trees thinned, and he came out upon the river-bank, where it was lighter under the open, already greying sky. Even so, it was difficult at first to make out anything except the blurred outline of the opposite bank, the dark water between and something which looked like a small island in mid-stream.

But it wasn't an island. Now that his eyes saw more clearly, Jack realized that this object was a wrecked aircraft, one smashed wing projecting upwards, like an arm out-stretched to summon help. And on that wing, in the faintly growing light, could be just made out the distinguishing mark of the Royal Air Force.

That decided Jack. Without more hesitation, he clambered down the bank and stood at the river's edge. He could see now that the machine had crashed upon a low sand-spit, only separated from where he stood by a narrow branch of the stream. How deep was it? He could only find that out by trying.

Jack waded in, knee-deep, waist-deep. For the last fifty yards or so, he was obliged to swim: then he was out of the water and close to the wrecked plane, a one-seater fighter, all twisted and crumpled by its impact, a heap of metal and plywood.

It had not caught fire; that was a big thing to be thankful for. But where was the pilot? Had he baled out and escaped? If so, what was the meaning of those shouts for help? They had certainly seemed to come from the direction of the derelict machine, and the problem of the missing airman must be solved somehow.

The dawn-light was strengthening: Jack began to search more carefully, and perhaps it was some sixth sense which impelled him to look upwards.

From behind a sort of cross-bar overhead he saw a leg protruding, a long leg wearing Air Force blue. But it was impossible to make out the rest of the body from where he stood.

The investigator proceeded to scramble up, precariously, over the tangled wreckage, impeded by the smashed and bent-back wing, which blocked his view. Not until he had negotiated this and found himself among the ruins of the fuselage was the owner of the leg visible.

He lay hunched up, pinned against the side of the cock-pit by broken parts of the machine, his head thrown back, his arms pressed tightly under him. In an instant Jack knew that the vague suspicions which had been growing in him ever since he saw that long blue-clad leg—perhaps still more vaguely, even before, when he heard those cries for help, were confirmed. For it was none other than Shanks who lay there.

He was lying very still, showing no sign of recognizing Jack, even of knowing that anyone was there. He hadn't moved—hadn't called out, since a long time before his would-be rescuer reached the wrecked machine.

Could he be dead—had Jack come too late to save his friend? No—that was too bad to be true.

"Shanks—Shanks!" he called aloud desperately. "Are you badly hurt, old chap?"

There was no answer, and Jack's heart sank still lower. He crawled a little closer, contrived to get his arms round the inanimate figure, trying to drag it free of the debris.

He could not manage this at the moment, but he succeeded beyond his hopes in another respect. For Shanks stirred, groaned, half-opened his eyes, then, as Jack gave another tug, uttered a smothered yell and a heartfelt stream of curses.

"Oh, Shanks, are you really alive?" Jack asked.

"Don't I sound like it?" Shanks retorted. "But I shan't be much longer, if you try to haul me out over umpteen knife-edges. Sure, you'll have all the skin flayed off my body!"

"I'm sorry. . . . I . . . I didn't know you could feel what I was doing, and I wanted to free you," Jack said penitently.

"Lucky for you that I'm *not* free!" Shanks ejaculated ungratefully. "I'd only just passed-out for a few minutes —got faint and dizzy, hanging head down like this, I suppose, and it didn't seem as if anyone was coming after me —even a Jerry. I had to risk that when I shouted. I suppose it really *is* you, Frere—seems so unlikely."

"It's me right enough."

"Thought I might be dead without knowing it. Well, for goodness' sake get me out of this. I'm all trussed up like a dead turkey."

5   (G 13)

" I'll have you out in a jiff," Jack promised optimistically.

It wasn't as easy as all that. There was plenty of sweating on Jack's part, plenty more swearing from The O'Morough-Ryan before the good work was accomplished and the airman freed. And even when he was clear of the wreckage, Jack had a horrible fear that he must be seriously injured in some way, for he did not seem able to move.

Shanks, however, soon reassured him.

" I don't believe any bones are broken: it's just cramp and stiffness. I've been pinned under there ever since we started back, escorting the last of the Whitley's. That's when I crashed—bad luck to me!—and it must be a good while ago."

" Quite five hours, I expect," Jack agreed. " P'raps if I rubbed you a bit it would help."

It did, although Shanks derided Jack's so-called gentle massage. Before very long he was able to move his limbs: after that, with Jack's help, it was a comparatively easy matter to reach the river-bank, just as the sun was rising, huge and red through layers of mist.

" It'll be a long time before *that's* got enough power to warm or dry us," Shanks said resentfully, as they stood cold and dripping by the river-side. " And what do we do next, I'd like to know?"

" Make for the rendezvous—although I don't suppose it will be much use," Jack answered.

" No, by jove!" Shanks stared in consternation. " You'll have missed the bus by coming back to help me."

" It doesn't matter——"

" It does, faith, and I'm an ungrateful swine. I suppose that crash knocked most of the senses out of me, or I'd have realized before what you'd done for me."

" It wasn't anything, Shanks—I'm only so tremendously glad that I happened to hear you shouting."

But Shanks was not to be consoled. As they made their way through the fir-forest, rather slowly and painfully, for the airman was still stiff and aching, he never ceased blaming himself and urging Jack to hurry on and let him manage for himself as well as he could.

"Leave you alone in Germany—is it likely, you blithering idiot?" Jack scoffed. "No, we're going to stick together whatever happens, so you may as well make up your mind to that. We can't be very far from the meeting-place now."

They were not, as Jack's map showed when they stopped to examine it a few minutes later. But from the point of view of a rendezvous, it might as well have been in the middle of the Sahara. Nothing but emptiness, silence, a silence which seemed to whisper "Too late".

CHAPTER XII

A Telephone Call

Even Shanks, with his usually powerful command of language, could find nothing to say at the moment.

The situation, mentally and bodily, was past words. Probably, for the time being, there was no British fighting force in which morale was lower. Jack was the first to speak.

"It's no good standing here to be spotted by the next Hun who passes," he said heavily. "Let's take cover."

A fair amount of this was provided by clumps of broom and heather, and after stumbling along for a few hundred yards, Shanks flung himself, face down, in the shelter of a thick bush.

"No use in going farther," he said. "Seems to me one place is as good as another in this cursed country, and we can't expect to hide long, anyway. Besides—I'm done. . . ."

Jack did not answer. He, too, lay down, his forehead resting on his arms, and tried to think out some plan. But it was useless. No thoughts or schemes would come, and he fell into a miserable uneasy doze.

A voice roused him.

" Here's your tea, sir."

So it had all been a bad dream, Jack thought drowsily. He was back in his camp billets, with Richards waking him just as usual. He rolled over with an effort, realizing as he did so that he lay on hard ground, that, overhead, pine-branches, shut out the open sky.

It wasn't only a nightmare then—but Richards stood there, a steaming mug of tea in each hand, beaming down at him.

" Have it while it's hot, Mr. Frere," he said maternally.

Jack dragged himself up into a sitting position.

" You know, you're not *really* here, Richards," he said. " It's completely and absolutely impossible."

" Not at all, sir. Have a biscuit."

" You're just a dream walking—you *must* be."

" Not at all, sir. Dear me, you're soaked through and through. I must get you into dry things as soon as possible."

" This tea isn't a dream anyway—at least, it *is*!"

" I put a little rum into it. You both looked as though you needed it, Mr. Frere."

" But where did it come from—and you too? How——"

" I'll tell you all about everything, sir, after you've had your tea, but *not* before," Richards said firmly.

Shanks, half roused and still looking dazed, was quite content at first to gulp down the hot liquid and ask no questions. But he made a quick recovery and was soon as eager as Jack to lie, drying and warming, in a patch of sun and listen to Richards' story.

" In the first place, how did you come to be left in Germany alone?" Jack demanded.

" Well, I'm not exactly alone, sir," Richards answered deprecatingly. " I've got a tank with me—a light tank."

" What?"

" Yes, sir, that's where the tea and everything came from. You see, that was the hush-hush job me and some others were trained for, driving and looking after light air-borne tanks, armed with a very special gun."

" By—Gosh!" Shanks stared, his eyes brilliantly blue with excitement. " *That* was kept secret."

" Very secret, sir. They landed us—a hundred tanks there were—with other British air-borne troops at this air-field the Dutch had seized and prepared for us just beyond the frontier, in Holland."

Richards went on to tell how they had waited there, until word came through by a runner that the raiding party had reached Schloss Schwartzigen. There the tanks, accompanied by supporting infantry, had crossed the frontier, within the section where loyal Dutch guerrilla troops had overpowered the German sentries and occupied the guard-houses, making and holding a clear passage for the British forces to reach the rendezvous, meet the paratroop commandos and return to the airfield and the troop-carrier.

" They were just grand, those Dutchmen," Richards declared enthusiastically. " Not even regular trained soldiers either, no uniforms and only weapons they'd managed to get hold of and hide, but brave as lions. And when they'd seen our fellows back across the frontier, they were just going to disperse, get back to their homes and wait for the next chance to have a go at the Huns."

" Richards," Jack said sternly. " Why didn't you and your tank go back with the rest this morning?"

For the first time Richards looked embarrassed.

" Well, sir," he reddened and hesitated. " You see, sir, I didn't see you at the rendezvous with the other para-

troops. So I felt a bit upset. But when I made a few inquiries, Mr. Gregory and several others told me you'd not
been scuppered, that you left the house with the rest of
them quite all right, not even wounded. So that made me
wonder what had become of you."

" And you determined to stay behind—desert, in fact?"

" Well, yes, sir. I couldn't make up my mind to leave
Germany without you," Richards answered.

" It's a most serious offence. You are liable to be shot
at dawn and . . . Hang it all, Richards, don't look so
confoundedly serious! You know I'm trying to say thank
you—but you oughtn't to have done it."

" I'm very glad I did, sir," Richards said sedately. " And
if it gave us a chance to do anything to help Captain Loring,
I'd be gladder still."

" I knew that was at the back of your mind," Jack said.
" But at the present moment I don't see a shadow of a chance
to help ourselves out of this hole, much less anyone else."

" Oh, between us we ought to be able to think of something." Shanks seemed to have regained his normal high
spirits as he stretched his lanky length in the sun, blinking
up at it, through half-closed eyes. " Where's this tank of
yours, Richards?"

" Not far away, sir—docked and camouflaged. I covered
it up with a lot of this green stuff, after I'd decided to stay.
In fact, I'd only just finished when you and Mr. Frere
turned up. So I watched where you went and thought I'd
surprise you with a nice cup of tea."

Consultation between the three showed a certain diver-
gence of opinion as to the next thing to be done. Shanks,
as was only natural after his ordeal, voted for a long sleep
till evening, hidden in cover. He argued, reasonably enough,
that it was impossible to risk appearing in daylight wearing
their present uniforms.

"We've got to get German clothes somehow," he said.

"As far as I can see the only way to do *that* is to take them from the S.S. men killed at Schloss Schwartzigen," Jack said. "And, if so, the sooner, the better, before the Huns discover what happened there. It's not 7 o'clock yet; with luck we can reach the Schloss and get away with what we want, before 8.0."

Shanks could not deny that this was their wisest course. They set off, then and there, Jack ahead as the only one who knew the way.

"Anyhow, I don't believe our uniforms could be spotted as British," Shanks declared, trying to rub off some of the sticky, stiffening mud, which encrusted his garments and was just beginning to dry as the sun's power increased.

They had met nobody as yet in the woods, except birds, beasts and insects. Coal-black squirrels, as well as the familiar red species, chased each other up and down the tree trunks like furry fairies, jays and wood-pigeons flew from branch to branch, and there was an incessant buzzing of flies and mosquitoes.

Otherwise silence, except for the unavoidable slight noises of their own progress through thickets and undergrowth, cracking of twigs, the swish of a bramble-trail.

At last Jack halted.

"We're close to the house," he whispered. "We mustn't make a sound now—for fear the alarm's been given already. Look here, I'd better go ahead and reconnoitre. Just a bit farther and we'll be able to see the front entrance: I'll signal from there if all's clear."

Soon Shanks and Richards were hidden in a thicket of rhododendrons, and the advance-guard of one set off alone, without much liking for his errand.

It was a strange and eerie experience. The Schloss might have been the enchanted palace of the spell-bound Princess, only with the sinister difference, that here it was that deeper, longer sleep of death which reigned supreme.

In the deserted grounds, Jack saw several of those sentries whom the raiders had first encountered. They lay sprawled upon the ground, or propped against trees, their uniforms dark and sodden with dew. One of them stared at Jack with wide open eyes, which seemed to challenge the intruder, but he passed on, moving more and more cautiously, through the front entrance and into the hall.

Here the same silence of death met him again, together with many signs that nothing had yet been discovered, no news of the raid had reached the outside world.

In the rooms and passages electric lights still burned behind the blacked-out windows. It was quite safe to give the signal which would bring his two friends to the house, and the sooner the better.

And then, before Jack could reach the front door, the silence of the house was broken by a sound which almost made him jump out of his skin. Into that place of death where nothing lived came the tinkle of a telephone-bell, the more uncanny because it was so prosaic.

Jack looked round wildly.

For the moment, he almost expected one of the dead men to rise up and answer the call. After all, it was meant for them.

Whoever listened at the other end of the wire, expected to make contact with the Secret Service Staff at the Schloss.

With that realization, Jack pulled himself together. If he took the call and reassured the caller, it might give him and his friends just the extra time they needed to get clear away. But if it wasn't answered, suspicions would certainly be roused, and they might be caught red-handed in the house.

There it was again, tinkling away impatiently. Jack ran

in the direction of the sound. He discovered the instrument in a small luxuriously-furnished office near the door, and took up the receiver.

"Heil Hitler," he said, in as guttural a voice as he could assume: "*Wo ist da?*—Who's there?"

"Heil Hitler! Is Herr General von Bockenburg there?" came the inquiry.

"No," Jack answered in his best German; the General was not yet up. He himself was the orderly officer.

"Ha-ha-ha!" came a chuckling laugh. "Not yet up, eh? What sort of a party last night? A bit *too* good, eh?"

"Yes, it was quite a good party," Jack managed to laugh naturally. "Even although the Führer wasn't there, the General enjoyed it."

"All's well with you, then?"

"Yes, all's well."

"And you know about the proceedings to-day at the Sports Arena? The great meeting at which the Führer has been announced to speak? Don't forget to tell the Herr General to bring as many of the staff with him as he can—for, of course, we expect him to come himself."

"Yes, of course. . . . What time is the meeting, exactly?" Jack asked.

"Three o'clock; well, you'll be there, you and all your friends. . . . Heil Hitler!"

Jack rang off and drew a long breath. He felt that he'd kept his end up pretty well. There'd been no trace of suspicion on the German's part.

All the same, there wasn't any time to waste. Telephone-calls meant also the possibility of visitors, a postman or a dispatch-rider might arrive at any minute.

Standing in the doorway, Jack waved imperatively and, at once Shanks and Richards appeared, making their way towards him.

During the strained twenty minutes which followed, Jack inwardly blessed, again and again, Richards' calm common sense. It was he who took charge of the proceedings, selected the most suitable uniforms for size, and brought them to the little office-room, to be fitted and adjusted to their owners. He even produced a small housewife and made a few alterations, tightening a collar, letting down a cuff.

" We don't want to have any little faults that can be put right, sir," he explained, when Shanks chafed at the delay. " We might meet a Hun officer and get pulled up for being wrongly dressed. Better give a bit more time to it now— there, that's a great improvement, Mr. Frere. Fits as if it had been made for you."

" There's that telephone again," Jack burst out feverishly.

For the irritating insistent tinkle had punctuated all their proceedings, and Jack had to force his brain to work quickly so as to sound convincing, when he answered the calls.

A wine merchant about his last order . . . other tradesmen —" It doesn't sound as if Government departments over here were so severely rationed as they make out!" Shanks interjected—then an ultra-official voice barking out questions about some new secret code and extremely put out because he could not speak personally to Major Dussel.

" I'm very sorry, Herr General," Jack felt it was good policy to assume the speaker was of a high rank. " But the major is busy—an important conference—I'll ask him to ring you up directly he is free. . . . Great Scott!"

Jack replaced the receiver and drew back, rubbing his ear, with a rueful grimace.

" What was it?" Shanks asked.

" The Hun at the other end gave a snort of annoyance like a mad elephant—nearly burst my ear-drum," Jack explained. " A little peevish with friend Dussel, I gather. What *are* you up to, Richards?"

" Well, your tunic still wanted a stitch or two, so I thought I'd better carry on while you were phoning. It's done now."

" Good! Then the sooner we get away the better—back to the tank. We'll take our own uniforms and bury them there—don't want to leave anything here to give ourselves away."

They all breathed more easily as they left that house of spectres and shadows: of staring eyes and the silence of death which the everyday tinkle of the telephone-bell only made more noticeable.

They heard it again as they hurried across the garden, and Jack found himself turning back automatically to answer the impatient summons.

" Here, don't be an ass." Shanks caught his sleeve, recalling him to himself.

" I've got it on the brain," Jack confessed, laughing. " I say, we must look quite a convincing Storm-troopers Three, if my get-up is as good as yours."

" Pass in a crowd with a push, I think," Shanks admitted. " Although my pants are too short."

" Well, none of them seemed to run to such long legs as you, sir," Richards apologized. " I did my best."

" And jolly good too—I'm not grousing, Richards. You're an absolute marvel—*and* the only one of us who really fits into his steel helmet."

" I've always been rather square-headed, sir: I suppose that's why. Anyhow, I don't think it much matters if we're seen now."

" But *not* heard," Jack grinned. " You'd both give yourselves away if you spoke a single word."

" Yes, it's a good thing you speak the lingo so well," Shanks allowed. " Otherwise we'd be in the soup up to our eyebrows."

They strode along the woodland paths confidently now,

three German soldiers to all appearances, bent on important military business. But they met no one except a couple of ancient wood-cutters, who muttered " Heil Hitler " as they passed, with no great show of enthusiasm.

Richards looked relieved when he found his tank undisturbed where he had left it, so cunningly branch-covered that it appeared part of the woodland landscape. He showed off its points proudly.

" Specially built for air transport—very light, very strong and the sweetest-tempered, easiest-driven A.F.V. I've ever handled," he said. " As for the gun—well, Mr. Frere, I ought not to have to tell *you* that it's the best of its kind in the world—bar none !"

" D'you mean—I say, Richards, is it really—you're not saying this is Captain Loring's gun?" Jack spoke excitedly.

" It is, sir." Richards fondled the short, thick muzzle lovingly. " Mounted on this tank for a practical test-out, which it hasn't had yet, not with the new secret projectiles. But there are a good many rounds here, in the tank . . . we *might* get a chance," Richards concluded wistfully.

" It's marvellous, Richards. No wonder you were a bit windy about that tank of yours. And now we'd better get these clothes well and truly buried before doing anything else."

This job took some time; it was necessary to dig deep, in case a wandering dog disinterred the incriminating garments.

Afterwards Richards prepared a meal of bully-beef and biscuit, which could be considered either a late breakfast or an early lunch, and it was while they were eating this that Shanks made his startling proposal.

They had been discussing possible plans without getting very much farther. Each idea seemed to come up short at the end of a blind alley, which led them nowhere, except to certain capture and imprisonment.

Shanks bitterly deplored the complete crash of his machine, for, to him as to other airmen, the only natural way to leave enemy territory was by air.

To distract his mind Jack told them again about that first telephone conversation at Schloss Schwartzigen, and how warmly he had been urged to attend Hitler's mass demonstration that afternoon without fail and with all his friends.

" I promised I would, too," he said, grinning at the aforesaid friends.

Shanks, sprawling on the sand, hands clasped behind his head, showed a sudden glint of vivid green-blue between his almost closed eyelids.

" Well, why not keep that promise?" he drawled. " Why shouldn't we—you and your friends—attend that meeting? Seems to me the most sensible plan we've struck yet."

CHAPTER XIII

Rendezvous with Hitler

For a moment Jack really wondered whether Shanks's crash had affected his brain. But the Irishman looked particularly calm and collected, not at all as though suffering from concussion or head injuries. Only in his eyes a danger signal glinted, that green light which did not mean all clear where The O'Morough-Ryan was concerned.

Richards goggled at the airman.

" Do you mean that, sir, or is it just one of your jokes?" he inquired mildly.

" Of course I mean it," Shanks retorted peevishly. " As we're in Germany, we want to make the most of it, don't we? See as much as we can of the country and the people. And it would be nothing less than criminal to miss such a chance of meeting the dear Führer."

"Especially as he funked our last appointment." Jack's tone was grim.

"Exactly so. I was just thinking of that," Shanks said reflectively. "Perhaps we could somehow make up for that little disappointment."

"Not much chance of another kidnapping stunt, I'm afraid."

"Perhaps not, but there are other ways of—what's that expression they use in Russia?—liquidating unpleasant people. I'm not a fanatic or particularly murderous-minded, but I'd love to feel I'd helped to rid the world of Adolf—even if it was the last thing I did on this earth."

"I'm with you there," Jack agreed gravely, and for a few moments all three sat silent. Under the lightness of his manner, Jack realized that Shanks hid a purpose sharp, strong and deadly as steel. He would laugh and joke up to the last moment, but, if the chance came, willingly sacrifice his own life to rid the world of an evil man, perhaps to save many thousands from death. Kill an enemy or save a friend —Ryan would not hesitate for an instant in either case.

Well, didn't he himself feel the same? And whatever they did would be fair and square open battle, with the odds thousands to three against them. A forlorn hope—that was the right name for it, and British soldiers had always been ready to volunteer for such adventures.

"What have you two got in the way of weapons?" Shanks inquired. "I've only my revolver."

"Grenades, knives, a Sten—not to mention Richards, with tank, cannon and Bren light machine-gun complete."

"Quite a hefty armament, but I'm afraid—like dogs— tanks aren't admitted to mass meetings! But we could use our A.F.V. to get to Drachem and, by the way, how far is it from here?"

"About forty miles, I believe. We'd have plenty of time.

But do you really think we could calmly drive across Germany in broad daylight on a British tank, as if it was a Green Line omnibus?"

"Why not? If anyone recognized it as British we—or rather you—you'd have to do all the talking—could say it was a captured tank. We certainly can't walk forty miles—and why should we, with a perfectly good conveyance *and* chauffeur? Besides, I'm sure Richards wouldn't leave it behind on any consideration."

"What shall we do with it when we get to Drachem?" Jack asked.

"Park it, or put it in the cloak-room: whatever they *do* do with tanks. Don't ask such simple questions."

The start of the momentous expedition was actually just as easy as Shanks made it sound. Richards brought out the tank, rubbed it up, gave it a look-over, and shook his head over the contents of the petrol-tank.

"Doubt if we'll have enough juice to take us to Drachem," he observed. "We might just do it, but only just."

"Oh, sufficient for the day—or the hour—or the five minutes ahead!" Shanks laughed recklessly. "Don't *look* for trouble, Richards. We're sure to find plenty, anyway."

"Well, sir, if we *did* happen to get hold of Hitler, we'd need the tank to take him off in a hurry——"

"You surely don't expect to do that, Richards?" Jack asked.

"You never know your luck, sir. It's best to be prepared for anything. We'll have to see if we can scrounge a little petrol somehow, from somewhere."

The sun shone brilliantly when they set out, making directly for the main road which, as shown on Jack's map, led to Drachem.

No lurking in woods or by-paths now. Three German soldiers were travelling openly through the German countryside. Richards was driving: Shanks sat by him inside the tank; Jack proudly perched in the open conning-tower, gazing around.

There was a pleasant smell of hay and pine-trees in the warm air. The few people they met did not seem much interested in them or their progress. After all, as Jack argued with himself, why should they be? Precious few in England would recognize a German tank *as* German, if it was driven by seemingly British soldiers. Rather an uncomfortable consideration, but true, and the same seemed to apply to Germany.

When they stopped for lunch on a stretch of heathy common, a little before noon, Shanks emerged from the tank wiping his brow.

" Phew, it's hot in there," he grumbled. " *And* boring. What I object to is the inactivity of the job. Might as well be pushed through the park in a perambulator like kids out with a nursemaid."

" You wouldn't have us trying to be spectacular, doing 'Action Front' or whatever manœuvres the Royal Tank Regiment perform on parade?" Jack inquired, but Shanks only shrugged his shoulders and demanded:

" What do you say, Richards? Didn't you find it as flat as a pancake? Don't you feel you want to do something?"

Richards was cautious and non-committal.

" I don't so much mind myself, sir," he said. " But I think that the little tank is somewhat disappointed. She thinks she's missing something in the way of excitement."

" I don't know about that," Jack said. " Seems to me there's something tremendously exciting in the feeling that we're three solitary invaders, the very first British mechanized land force in this war to drive a spear-head so far into Germany's very heart."

" Hark to him!" Shanks declaimed. " 'We were the

first, That ever burst into that silent sea—' or, rather, the sacred precincts, the Holy of Holies, where the Führer reigns as a deity."

"Oh, you may laugh," Jack looked rather self-conscious. "But it's jolly thrilling all the same."

Shanks fell silent, chewing a grass-stalk, glancing sideways at Jack's flushed excited face. He himself had far too much imagination not to share his friend's feelings, and Richards' remark about the tank had caught his fancy. He looked at the little fighting vehicle now, standing there on the sun-dried grass, an expanse of purple heather stretching away behind, and thought it was for all the world like a British lion cub, crouched there defiant and calling upon all enemies to come on and be attacked if they dare.

Yet the landscape showed no sign of war as far as the eye could reach: there was no roar of battle or rattle of machine-guns. Here was a British fighting force in the enemy's country—unopposed.

As though feeling this in every drop of its petrol, the tank pounded along most valiantly when they started again after lunch, bouncing on its tracks, its gun poked up aggressively. And, as it turned out, there was to be no lack of adventure during this next lap of the journey: rather more indeed than was altogether desirable.

It began when they swung round a bend and came upon a small German army one-seater car drawn up on the grass road-verge, with a hotly perspiring German officer burrowing into its internals and only visible from the waist downwards in consequence.

He looked round as the tank rolled up alongside and mopped at his forehead. Seeing Jack perched aloft, he snapped out peremptorily, even forgetting the usual "Heil Hitler" formula:

"Here, you fellows can help me."

"What's the matter, Herr Hauptmann?" Jack had noticed the captain's rank marks.

"Shouldn't need your help if I knew. . . The confounded car petered out, and I can't get it to move, though I've been tinkering at it for an hour. Here, don't sit there staring at me—get to work," the German ended ungraciously.

Jack knew that, in the character of a German soldier, he dared not show the slightest hesitation in obeying this order from an officer. He climbed out of the tank, summoned Richards, and managed to give him instructions in an undertone, telling him to find out, if he could, what was the matter with the car.

Meanwhile the German captain, plainly glad to be relieved from his task, walked over to the tank.

"Hullo!" he put up a black-rimmed monocle and stared suspiciously. "What's this—an English tank?"

Fortunately Jack was ready for this question, and his German fluent.

"Yes, Herr Hauptmann. It's one we captured in that last raid on Dieppe," he said glibly. "A quite new type it is, for use with airborne troops. I and my two mates here had orders to study its mechanism thoroughly, then take it for a little tour round this district, stopping at the different villages to give demonstrations."

"To show the folk what a British tank looks like in case of invasion, eh?" Captain Frölich laughed boisterously. "That's really a good joke—but we Germans are prepared for every contingency, even the most unlikely."

Jack, although relieved at the way in which his story had been received, wondered what was to be done if this unpleasant type turned suspicious again. Of course, the three of them in an emergency could tackle him, but he was an ugly customer, with his duel-scarred face, loose mouth and piggish eyes.

Richards now made signs to Jack, who managed to disengage himself and join the other by the car. In undertones, Richards explained that he couldn't put the matter right: something was radically amiss, and garage attention would be needed.

On hearing this from Jack, Herr Hauptmann Frölich lost his temper completely.

" What's the use of sending a fellow round to explain British tanks, if he can't do simple running repairs for a good German car?" he stormed. " Here—let *me* talk to him !"

" I'm afraid it isn't much use, Herr Hauptmann, unless you understand the Czech language," Jack plunged boldly and desperately. " My comrade, Wilhelm Heck, is one of the Sudeten Germans."

" Then he might as well be a double Dutchman for me ! All these foreigners chucked into our army. . . . Then what am I going to do? It is urgently necessary that I should get to Drachem in time for the mass meeting this afternoon."

" We are going with the tank to Drachem too, Herr Hauptmann," Jack said.

" Good! Then you can take me also with you." The officer puffed with relief, his furrowed brow relaxed.

" Willingly, Herr Hauptmann," Jack agreed, but when through one of the apertures, he communicated this plan to Shanks in a whisper, the interior of the tank became even more sultry and sulphurous than before.

" What the—how the—why the—Couldn't you have put the brute off? It's just asking for trouble."

" You're wrong there. He'll make an excellent passport to take us into Drachem, besides wangling the petrol we need to get there. Richards says we shouldn't have pulled it off otherwise. Just keep quiet and we'll worry through somehow.   Remember you and Richards are both Czechs and don't understand a word of ordinary German."

All the same, the rest of that journey was rather like sitting on an escape valve or the entrance to a wasp's nest and hoping for the best, while fearing the worst. The captain barked out incessant questions regarding the tank, many of which Jack—not being a tank technician—found it very difficult to answer. He could not pass the queries on to Richards, since it was impossible to address him in English, which the German would certainly recognize. There was a slight diversion while they filled up with petrol at a roadside garage, but Jack sighed with relief when they came at last to the crest of a ridge of low hills and saw below them in a vast shallow saucer the great munitions centre of Drachem, with its huge factory blocks, its chimneys, and buildings, stretching in all directions, under a yellowish-grey pall of smoke, blotting out patchily the blue of the summer sky.

" In case you do not know it, the Sports Arena, where the mass meeting is to take place, is on the far side of the town from here, nearest the Forest—the Drachem-Wald," Captain Frölich said importantly. "You had better skirt round the suburbs—there is a fine circular road—then you will be able to drop me at the entrance to the arena. We have still plenty of time before the ceremonies begin."

These instructions were duly obeyed, and Herr Hauptmann Frölich deposited with all due pomp and ceremony before a Swastika-decorated archway, through which streams of people were steadily passing.

Jack's salute in parting was almost over realistic, as Shanks informed him, when they had driven on a few miles into the Drachemwald, to seek a hiding-place for the tank in one of its lonely glades or gorges.

" You're getting altogether too, too Hitler-youthful, my

lad," the Irishman said. "That's the way Quislings are made, by imitating the real thing."

"If you only knew how utterly sick I feel every time I say 'Heil Hitler', you'd not make a joke of it. . . . I say, Richards, what price this for a hidey-hole, might have been made for us?"

They had reached a steep, rocky cliff, overgrown with trees and shrubs, which had been quarried at some former time. Jack noticed one of these excavations, tangled over with brambles into which a sloping path led down. It was the very place they needed, near the main road, easily accessible, yet well hidden. If they erased all tracks carefully and covered the tank with foliage, it was a thousand to one against its being found.

It did not take long to stow the tank away in this safe harbour and obliterate the marks of its tyres and their own footprints on the dry sandy paths leading to the excavation.

Then the three set off on foot in the direction of the Sports Stadium, trying rather unsuccessfully to discuss future plans as they went, since obviously they would not be able to talk together in English later on, when surrounded by German ears.

"All the same it's no good. We can't settle anything; we'll just have to wait and see what happens—trust to luck," Jack said at last.

"Well, it's been with us so far," Shanks answered. "We can't complain. What's up, Richards? You look as though you'd just lost a pound note and found sixpence."

"As a matter of fact, sir, it is a question of finance that's bothering me," Richards replied. "I was just wondering what we're to do about the charge for admission to this affair. We've not got any German money."

"No, by gosh, you're right! that is a problem. How about it, Shanks?"

" We'll just have to trust to luck again," the Irishman answered, and as it happened his trust was justified.

When they reached the entrance to the arena and joined the stream of people passing in, it was to find that admission was free. No one took any notice of them in that crowd of mixed soldiers and civilians, these last mostly factory workers and a haggard weary-looking company in the main.

There was no lack of material efforts to cheer and inspire them. Bands crashed out military and operatic music at intervals from platforms on every side of the huge arena, loud-speakers bawled encouragement, broadcasting addresses from Goering, Goebbels and other leaders of the Reich.

" No German citizen need fear hunger during the coming season," promised the burly leader of the Luftwaffe, with his assumed air of bluff good humour. " You will be well fed, every one of you on supplies from the conquered countries—Danish butter, Norwegian salmon, French rolls, Russian caviare—perhaps English bacon and eggs if you're very good——"

Roars of laughter responded to this from the ranks of Storm troopers on either side of the raised dais—at present empty—on one side of the stadium, the place from which Hitler was evidently to speak later and behind which hung a Swastika-adorned banner of gigantic proportions, supported by two immense gilded eagles.

But the factory workers did not seem to be particularly cheered by Goering's glowing visions; they remained solemn and silent on the whole. Neither were they much more responsive when Dr. Goebbels took the air, with a blood-curdling account of the latest British atrocities invented for the occasion.

Again the Storm troopers cheered and shouted. Yells of " Gott Strafe England!" rose again and again, an ugly sound which Jack thought must be rather like the howling of wolves on a blood-trail.

Then a stout man with a microphone and a conductor's baton started community choruses, the inevitable *Horst Wessel* song, another with the stirring refrain " We are marching on England."

" Don't think much of this performance," Shanks said almost without moving his lips. " And I'd always heard the Huns were such a musical people!"

To Jack it all sounded forced: some of the workers near him were singing, but in a mechanical way, as if they had been drilled.

" I suppose it will be different when Hitler himself appears," he thought. " One has always heard about his extraordinary magnetic effect on audiences. And it seems to me that something is going to happen pretty soon. There's a sort of feeling of excitement working up and those young Nazis over there seem to be a kind of Guard of Honour getting ready to receive him."

At that moment a tremendous blare of brass instruments burst out, as six trumpeters performed an elaborate fanfare. A door opened at the back of the dais, with its overhanging Swastika, and the Nazi guard of honour formed up on either side in double ranks.

Two figures appeared in the entrance, and instantaneously the guard of honour thrust up their arms stiffly with a roared-out: " Heil Hitler!"

But almost before Jack could take in what he was seeing, he heard Richards at his elbow give a startled exclamation, felt him grip his arm fiercely.

" Look—look, sir," he gasped.

Jack was already looking. Once again Hitler had disappointed expectations—but that was not all. For the two figures on the platform were Max von Kressen and Peter Loring.

CHAPTER XIV

In the Trap

Not only the three onlookers were taken aback. Although for different reasons, the whole assembly was bewildered. Expecting the Führer in person, the two figures on the platform heralded with so much pomp and circumstance, were an anticlimax to say the least of it and, after the first automatic salutes and cheers had been given, this feeling was shown plainly enough.

Murmurs rose, a kind of buzz and hum with an almost threatening undertone. It brought about an infiltration of sinister figures; the uniformed Gestapo police moving here and there in the crowd, vigilant, deadly. At sight of them order was restored momentarily, but in their wake, mutterings began again.

But Max von Kressen was too clever a man not to sense the atmosphere of dissatisfaction. He strode forward to the front of the platform, and his voice rang out, dominating the doubtful crowd, persuading, even while apologizing for his presence.

" I know, friends, that you are disappointed, seeing me here in the place of our leader. . . . I share in that disappointment myself. . . . But the Führer is absent for no selfish, no personal reason, as I know, who am honoured by being in his confidence, however unworthy of such a high place. . . . A call came to him from our armies at the Front, and he obeyed it. The commander-in-chief of the Reich is always at the command of his soldiers, as you and I know.

" So he appointed me to bring you his message, and if the lips that speak are mine, the words are those of our beloved Führer himself. . . ."

" The chap seems to need quite a lot of words to tell his audience that dear Adolf has cold feet," Shanks observed.

Jack nodded. His first surprise over, with Richards still staring dumbly, clutching his arm in a convulsive grip, he had managed to convey to the Irishman Loring's identity, and the fact that von Kressen was one of the chief Nazi leaders, Hitler's right-hand man.

Now, one idea possessed Jack, to get closer to the platform, so as to make communication with Peter at least remotely possible. Even at the risk of attracting the attention of von Kressen, this must be done: after all, the Man in Brown might not recognize him in disguise, and he would scarcely know Richards again.

Shanks was ready for anything which promised action, and they began to edge a way through the close-packed throng, inch by inch, in a succession of movements, which brought them in course of time quite near to the dais.

It was becoming more and more evident that something was radically wrong with the meeting. Music and words were not having their usual emotional effect; both seemed irrelevant.

For these workmen and factory hands, people from the industrial areas devastated by the British, had come for solace, for assurance that the bombing of these districts would cease and that reprisals would be taken against the enemy. They asked for bread in the shape of comfort and were given a stone—however eloquently delivered by the Führer's deputy.

Music was no more soothing in its effect. Attempts to start community singing failed: there were disjointed bursts here and there, but none of them whole-hearted, more the kind of broken-off choruses which soldiers might indulge in when cleaning equipment, or cavalrymen in grooming their horses.

There were no such full-throated roarings of the *Wacht am Rhein* or other patriotic songs, as those which generally distinguished these assemblies: there were even a few derisive cat-calls and whistles through the fingers, with broken snatches of somewhat ribald street-songs, which made the Gestapo police scowl and move towards the offenders menacingly.

Altogether there was plenty of discordant noise going on; enough to drown the rapid exchange of low-voiced remarks in English between Jack and Shanks—enough to prevent another sound from being over-noticeable, a sound which also came from that little group of intruders.

Richards had followed close behind his two companions, as they manœuvred a passage through that enemy mine-field of massed humanity, scarcely knowing what he did, or where, moving like a mechanical figure, he went.

That clutching at Jack's arm had been almost unconscious: Richards' usually well-behaved and orderly mind was still struggling in bewilderment, trying to grasp the new situation.

All had happened so suddenly and unexpectedly, even although his hopes and efforts, since Peter Loring's disappearance and the discovery that he was in Germany, had been concentrated upon reaching that country himself.

Now, he was not only in the same country, but within a few hundred yards of Loring in the flesh. Not too much flesh, though: not nearly enough. Richards' heart ached as he saw how thin and drawn and haggard the captain looked; for the moment he forgot all other considerations.

" He wants feeding up and looking after, same as I always did when we were together. He'd never think of himself, not even change his things if he was soaked through and through. But he doesn't even know I'm here, and I can't think of any way to tell him."

Richards felt rather as a faithful dog must when unable to let his master know of his presence, or his longing to help and save him, if only he could, from any danger or any enemies.

Dumb and helpless, he dared not call out or make any sign. He retained enough of his wits to warn him that such action would be dangerous, as much to Loring as himself. And although by means of an intensely concentrated stare he tried to will the captain to look his way, the effort was unsuccessful.

Jack turned and whispered a few words, but Richards scarcely heard what he said, certainly did not grasp the sense of it. So he did not try to answer, only nodded his head dumbly and continued to push on through the crowd, content that every step in this direction brought him a little nearer to the captain.

All sorts of nonsense buzzed in his brain. What was that Mr. Frere had said, back in England, that day they first talked about getting over to Germany? Something about a crooner chap, called Blondell or Blondin or some such name, wasn't it, who'd gone about looking for his master, King Richard, and managed to find out where he was imprisoned, as well as let the King know he was there, by singing a tune they both knew well.

Mr. Frere only meant it as a joke of course—just laughing he'd been, in that nice sort of way he had. But, all the same mightn't there be something in it, mightn't it be a way? One would have to be careful though: no ordinary English tune would be safe, like " Tipperary " or " Rule Britannia ".

They were quite close to the platform now: only a few rows of heads separated them from the black-and-gold draperies which hung round it. Richards could see all the figures upon it clearly—S.S. men in sombre black uniforms; high-up officials, looking too tightly buttoned-up:

that man in a brown suit, who'd come instead of Hitler, talking away sixteen to the dozen.

Mr. Frere was saying something about him just now, but Richards hadn't caught it: nor had he concentrated upon the man enough to recognize in him the visitor who had carried Peter Loring away. Truth to tell, Richards had no eyes or thoughts except for the captain himself.

He was wearing the same grey suit he'd gone away in: he stood there very straight and erect, staring straight in front of him, as if he wasn't much interested in anything or anybody.

" If I could only make him look at me," Richards thought —and was suddenly inspired by the memory of something which might do the trick.

That little tune—sort of Christmas carol thing—the captain was so fond of. He'd got in the way of whistling it every morning, after he'd had his bath, to warn Richards he would soon be ready for breakfast. It was German, too, so it wouldn't sound out of the way to these Huns all round him, even if they noticed one chap whistling, with all this noise going on.

Very softly at first Richards began to whistle that haunting little air: " Holy night, peaceful night." He repeated it, more boldly this time as he gained confidence, and one or two of those nearest to them glanced round, although with no special interest. Only Jack turned with a frown and a muttered " Shs' ", thinking that Richards must have gone suddenly mad.

But he showed no particular signs of craziness, only went on whistling his tune clearly and sweetly, with his eyes fixed on Peter Loring. And then Jack saw that Peter's head had turned slightly, that he was looking in their direction— knew that he had recognized Richards and himself.

Loring's pale cheeks flushed slightly, his eyes seemed to

come to life. For just a second Jack saw the old Peter, the Peter he knew. Then the lips set stiffly again and the eyes hardened as Loring muttered a few words to von Kressen.

The Man in Brown did not even look round, but a flicker of triumph passed over his face, which gave Jack a sick powerless feeling. It was as though Peter himself had betrayed them to the enemy.

"Did you see, Mr. Frere, did you see?" Richards' whisper, hissed into his ear, broke in on Jack's thoughts. "The captain heard me—he saw us!"

"What good is that? It was a mad thing to do, Richards."

"We must rescue him, sir—get him away somehow. There's the tank. If he'd lend a hand himself—manage to slip off. Couldn't you speak to him, Mr. Frere?" Richards asked feverishly.

Von Kressen was speaking again, trying to hold the attention of an audience which was growing noisier and more unruly every minute, making it quite possible to carry on even an English conversation in undertones without much risk.

Rather unexpectedly Shanks supported Richards.

"Yes, Jack, I think you ought to try to get a word with Loring," he said, speaking out of the side of his mouth, so that the Germans round might not overhear. "It's only fair to ourselves and him, since we *are* here. After all, he may have some plan of escape."

Jack shrugged his shoulders hopelessly: he felt too sick at heart to tell the others that he had himself seen Peter point out their presence to the Man in Brown. He would just do as they said, try to get a word with his cousin, whatever the result might be. Things could not be worse than they were, and if they made the first move, Fate might perhaps take a hand to overcome the apparently insuperable tangle of barbed-wire obstacles.

Anyhow, it was no good hesitating any longer. There couldn't be a better chance than now, while von Kressen was speaking. Jack began to shoulder his way nearer and nearer to the dais, with Shanks and Richards close beside him.

Some of those whom they pushed aside glared and grumbled. One workman protested angrily. " Here, who are you shoving? You soldiers think you're everybody!"

" Pardon, friend," Jack tried to be conciliatory. " We've a message to give, an important message to one of those there on the platform, which won't wait."

Still muttering, the man made way. Jack and his companions had now nothing between them and the platform; they were within half a dozen yards of the place where Peter Loring stood. But he showed no sign of being aware of their presence and still wore that remote air.

" Peter!" Jack spoke in the softest of whispers, yet it seemed to him that his voice echoed out, loud and raucous. Changing his first intention, he went on in German. " We're here, Peter. Won't you—can't you come with us—leave this place?"

Without moving a muscle of his face or body, Loring answered in a curious flat voice, like that of a ventriloquist.

" I cannot come. You had better go away at once—if it is still possible."

" We won't go without you." Having actual speech with his cousin had strengthened Jack's resolution. " Don't you want to help yourself and us?"

Peter Loring shook his head almost imperceptibly, but very decisively, and at that Richards burst out in a frantic undertone.

" Oh, sir, don't look like that. We *can't* leave you . . . not after coming so far."

This time the desperation in Richards' voice, as well as

the unfamiliar language, attracted attention. Several of those on the platform glanced round suspiciously, and it did not help matters when Shanks lost his easily-mislaid temper and muttered angrily to Jack.

"It's no use—waste of breath! It's only what we might have expected from him. It looks as if you were wrong all along thinking he's here in Germany unwillingly."

It was at this instant that von Kressen broke off his speech and swung round, making Jack feel at once that all was up. The strange red-fringed eyes took in the whole scene, seemed to understand all its implications in the flicker of an eyelid.

He spoke sharply.

"What is it? What do you men want?"

"You know very well," Jack answered firmly. "We want Captain Loring."

It was a relief to put a plain fact into words, to feel that it didn't matter any longer what he said. Yet he wasn't prepared for the effects of these words upon von Kressen.

The Man in Brown stiffened: his features sharpened wolfishly, his eyes glared with rage. He made a movement forward with hand raised, as though he would have struck Jack, who swerved aside, startled by this sudden change from the persuasive orator to a man whose face was distorted with fury.

"You dare to say such a thing as that to me!" von Kressen shouted in German. "What are soldiers of the Reich coming to that you enter this place openly boasting of such a vile purpose. Murder—assassination—the shedding of innocent blood by ignorant scoundrels! Ach! take that hand out of your pocket—you've some hidden weapon there, I'll be bound." He gripped Jack's wrist, and as he dragged him roughly backward, shouted a string of orders.

At once, as though by magic, the Gestapo police swarmed

up on to the platform from all sides, surrounding the three British soldiers, grasping their arms, thrusting hands into their pockets in search of weapons, doing it all with brutal thoroughness.

There was obviously no use in attempting to resist them, although Shanks was white with sheer fury, his eyes snapping green like those of a trapped leopard.

"You see that they are armed to the very teeth?" von Kressen turned back to the audience with a dramatic gesture, holding up the trench knife which had just been taken from Jack's belt. "With butchers' weapons such as these—with grenades and revolvers!—and why did they come here prepared for slaughter in such a fashion? I will tell you!"

The speaker was holding the full attention of his big audience now, there was no doubt of that. An almost breathless silence prevailed as he went on, his voice rough and grating with anger and indignation.

"It is right you should hear the whole truth, German workers, German soldiers, that you should know what might have happened, would have happened, but for the presence of mind and quickness of their intended victim. He saved his own life and mine also, for I have no doubt that I was to be included, by recognizing these men in time. What was their aim—to murder in cold blood one who has proved himself a loyal friend to the Reich, who has rendered Germany, our country, great and most valuable services. You know him, all of you, although perhaps not by sight, as 'Captain Peter', whose broadcast voice has spoken, night after night, telling the whole world the whole truth about Germany."

Von Kressen was interrupted by an outburst of applause and cheering. It would appear that "Captain Peter" was a popular character with the crowd.

"And why did they plan this hateful crime?" the speaker

went on. "Merely because he was born in England—although he has long been spiritually with us Germans, heart and soul, in sympathy with all our hopes. That he is English is surely no reason to wish and attempt his death —we should admire his bravery, loyalty and sincerity all the more, for what he has given up. He is branded as a traitor in his own country—for Germany's sake! His British friends and relations have disowned him—for Germany's sake! And what was to be his reward? Death at the hand of a German soldier!"

This time the interruptions took a far fiercer and louder form than before, shouts of "Shame!" hisses, catcalls, a rising roar of "heil—heil Hauptmann Peter!"

Again von Kressen made himself heard, and now his voice had an almost persuasive note, purring as well as raging.

"I am glad that you are shocked, friends—that you do not support these rascals who have disgraced the uniform of the Reich. For they were insolent enough to think that many here would do that—they actually demanded that Captain Peter should be handed over to them, there and then. Could one have believed that any calling themselves Germans would be so vilely treacherous to their friends, to one who is known too as the friend of the Führer himself, chosen to accompany me here to-day to speak to you in the Führer's place and in the Führer's name."

Again came the angry shouts, the cries of: "Heil Hitler!" —"Heil Captain Peter!" accompanied by a low angry murmur, very ugly to hear, with fists shaken at the three prisoners.

"They shall pay for their treachery, you can be sure of that," von Kressen promised his audience, and turned again to address the Gestapo police.

"Take these men into custody," he said. "I myself

6   (G 13)

will be answerable for them to the military authorities and
to the Führer. These are my orders, that they shall be kept
under close guard in the Klosters prison and not allowed to
communicate with their relations, families or regimental
comrades on any account whatever. I may interrogate
them myself later, or leave it to the Gestapo."

Jack hurriedly translated what the speaker had said to his
companions, and they stared at each other blankly. Here
was about the strangest state of affairs imaginable—that
they should be arrested and imprisoned as German soldiers,
for a supposed attempt to assassinate Peter Loring. Topsy-
turvey wasn't the word for it: it seemed altogether mad,
especially as von Kressen himself certainly knew who Jack
and Richards really were.

The Gestapo police were already beginning to hustle
them roughly away towards the back of the platform, when
Jack made one last appeal to his cousin, standing there
stiffly aloof, as though all this did not concern him in the
least degree.

" You can't let this happen to us, Peter; you know we
meant you no harm, that it is all a lie or a mistake,"—
difficult to say anything that he wanted to in German, yet
it would have been far too dangerous to speak English.

In any case it was useless. Peter stared at him coldly with
no recognition in his eyes.

" I know nothing about you at all," he said, " and I
cannot interfere. You will have plenty of opportunity to
explain your intentions. It is no business of mine."

There was no time for any more. They were already at
the top of the steps leading to a passage behind the dais,
which, in its turn, opened upon the street. From outside
came that same sinister murmur of many voices to which
von Kressen's speech had stirred the audience in the arena.
Evidently a crowd had gathered round the door to see the

prisoners brought out, and the crowd was in a most unpleasant temper.

Even the Gestapo men looked at each other rather uneasily.

" Herr von Kressen and the Führer himself will be angry if anything happens to them before they've been questioned," one of them muttered. Another shrugged his shoulders.

" The crowd's in a nasty mood. We'll have a job to protect them," he said. " Here—some of you men go out first and make a passage to the car."

Grasping the situation, Shanks glanced sideways at Jack, with a dangerous light in his eyes.

" I don't like being lynched by that filthy mob out there as a Hun soldier with an extra-special dislike of the British —in fact, I'd simply hate it," he said. " How about telling 'em who we really are? There'd be much more satisfaction in crashing, if we were flying our own colours."

But Jack shook his head.

" I know exactly how you feel, and I absolutely agree," he said. " But I don't think we'd better give out anything yet—it's not the right moment somehow. Time enough if it's a question of a court martial or anything of that kind —then it is bound to come out."

For a moment Shanks looked obstinate; then he gave in, although sulkily, and made no move to reveal their identity as the Gestapo men jostled them through the open door and closed round to safeguard them into the waiting police car.

There was a positive roar from the crowd as they emerged; arms waved, women spat like vicious cats, men yelled and cursed, surging forward, trying to break through the ring of guards and get at the prisoners.

Things looked and sounded extremely nasty. Stones and other missiles were flung, and although their steel helmets

protected them to some extent, Jack was soon bleeding from
a cut lip, and Richards from a nasty gash across the cheek.
It would have gone far worse with them had the mob got
their way, but the Gestapo police stuck to their prey doggedly, and once they had been thrust into the big black
closed car, the chauffeur was ordered to drive on regardless
of anyone who might try to impede him, a rough and ready
way of clearing the way, which was successful.

Once clear of the Sports Stadium they went at a tremendous pace, taking the same road which the three had followed, before hiding the tank that morning. But they did
not go as far; before reaching the outskirts of the forest,
the driver turned off through double gates and drew up
before a large bleak-looking building, which was recognizable at once as a prison.

"Talk about 'All hope abandon ye who enter here',"
Shanks muttered, as they passed in under the grim archway, but to Jack it seemed that the moment of complete
despair only came when a heavy door clanged upon them
and a key turned in the lock with a horrible well-oiled
slickness, somehow much more intimidating than if it had
grated rustily.

They were in a narrow, white-washed cell, with a minute
barred window, more than six feet above floor-level and a
three-tiered bunk along one wall. That was all, except for
a wooden bench clamped to the ground.

The three avoided each other's eyes as they sat down:
there seemed nothing to say, or, at least, no words to express
what they felt at that moment.

CHAPTER XV

Done Brown

"It's a black look-out," Shanks remarked.

"Couldn't well be worse, but you said just now that we ought to try and see the bright side," Jack pointed out irritably. "Do be consistent."

"I am only referring to the so-called meal that shaven-headed, pig-eyed Hun soldier thrust upon us a few minutes ago," Shanks explained. "Black-rye bread, a black-pudding of a sausage, and the blackest so-called coffee I ever set eyes on. No milk, and heaven only knows what it's made of—certainly not coffee beans!"

"What does it matter? *I* certainly don't feel like eating anything," Jack said miserably.

"That's where you're wrong." The Irishman had seated himself beside the tray which the German private had deposited on the end of the bench, and spoke with his mouth full. "I'm not saying it's good food—in fact, it's definitely beastly, but we've had nothing except a snack for twelve hours or so, and I'm hungrier than I thought I was. You'll find the same if you try."

"I don't want anything," Jack repeated doggedly.

"Better do as Mr. Ryan says, sir." Richards had followed Shanks's example. "There's no knowing when we'll be given anything else, and we mustn't let 'em get us down too low. We'll need all our strength."

Jack felt ashamed of his own gloom, when he caught Richards' solicitous gaze, saw the Irishman's cheerful grin.

"You're a good chap, Shanks—and you're quite right," he muttered, edging along the bench to join them. "It's an awful shame to have dragged you into this mess."

" Why, where else should I be, unless it's in the jam you got me out of?" Shanks asked. " Mind you, I'm not saying our prospects are bright, but I suppose almost anything in the world *might* be worse."

Might it? Jack wondered, although he did not put the thought into words, as he gnawed an unyielding crust of rye-bread. The Gestapo trap had closed upon them, and it was not likely to open its jaws easily. And Peter, with the help of von Kressen, had pushed them into it: that was the thing which hurt most.

To confess their real identity, to claim to be treated as British prisoners of war was not likely to help them either, all the more because they would certainly be identified at once with the happenings at Schloss Schwartzigen and reprisals taken accordingly.

It was nearly eleven o'clock at night. The cell was lit by a single glaring, unshaded electric light, and the prisoners had had no visitors except the German private who brought the tray of food.

Yet none of them felt inclined to turn in on the uninviting bunks; each had a feeling that something might happen at any moment—and they were right.

There came the thud of heavy footfalls along the stone corridor, a voice giving abrupt concise orders, at the sound of which Jack frowned and bit his lip. He had heard that voice before in such strangely different circumstances and places.

" Heil Hitler!" It was speaking again. " I wish to interrogate the prisoners, Herr Commandant. Do you wish to see the Führer's authority?"

" No, indeed, gnädige Herr: your own authority is enough." It was hard to believe that those dulcet tones came from the prison commandant, whose blue jowl, pouched bleary eyes and revoltingly brutal manner had vividly impressed themselves on the prisoners during a brief interview five or six hours before.

"Good! Is this the cell? The sentries can remain on guard at both ends of the corridor, in case I should want them. There is no need for one outside the door."

The well-oiled key turned in the lock; the door swung open. Max von Kressen and Peter Loring entered, and it was closed behind them. Both wore long dark military overcoats covering them to the heels, and soft German service caps, but it was not only their dress which had been changed from the civilian garments of the afternoon. These seemed almost like different men, and the surprising transformation did not end there.

Von Kressen spoke first in rapid English.

"There isn't time to give all the explanations needed now: most of that must wait until afterwards. For the moment, the only thing that matters is to get away—all of us."

"*All* of us!" Jack stared blankly.

"Yes—to England."

"To England!" Again Jack found himself repeating what seemed to him stupid meaningless words.

"That surprises you, eh?" von Kressen laughed outright at Jack's expression, then caught himself up, with a glance at Peter Loring, which made him look almost boyish. "It would hardly do if we were heard laughing with our prisoners. . . ." The face returned to gravity. "But I can assure you, Mr. Frere, that I am in greater danger than any of you."

"*You!*" Jack echoed.

"I hardly expect you to believe me—yet. Loring, perhaps they're more likely to take your word for it than mine, and as it's necessary that they should trust me . . . "

"Briefly, it's like this," Peter Loring took up the story.

" Max von Kressen, friend of the Führer, Nazi leader, jew-baiter and Britain-hater has a reverse side. He's also Hitler's bitterest enemy, strongest of anti-Nazis, staunch supporter of the Allies and their aims. He had managed to lead this double life, play this double part for a long time, but now he's gone too far at last. It's a matter of hours only now before he's discovered for what he is . . . by the Gestapo."

" And you, Peter?" Jack asked.

" Oh, I'm in the same boat—here in Germany to help him and the Allied cause—*and* in the same danger of discovery. You shall hear everything later if we've the luck to escape: that's going to take us all our time. So will you trust von Kressen and myself? I think I can ask it of you and Richards, Jack, old boy—in spite of my apparent appalling callousness this afternoon."

" Of course you can," Jack said emphatically, while Richards burst out: " You don't need to ask, sir—you *know*!"

" As far as I'm concerned, too, what Jack and Richards says goes," Shanks drawled.

" Good! Then we can get to work," von Kressen said. " Here's the plan roughly. For a long time I've known that I should need a quick means of getting away sooner or later. So in the Drachemwald, deep in the forest, not many miles from here, I've kept an aeroplane in a hidden hangar always ready, with a mechanic in charge. He's a completely dependable man, and can pilot the machine if necessary."

" So can I for that matter," Shanks grinned.

" Good! When I ordered them to bring you to this place, I had it in mind that it was on the outskirts of the town, nearest to the forest. What I propose is to take you away with me in the car that is waiting outside—ostensibly to transfer you to another prison for further interrogation. I think that excuse will satisfy the commandant. Actually, of course, we make for the forest and the hidden hangar. The chauffeur is another completely trustworthy fellow."

" You may as well add that if we get away without a fight we'll be lucky," Peter Loring commented. " You've taken big risks, cut things pretty close, von Kressen; there's no doubt now that the Gestapo have traced the big leakage of information to us, and if, as we suspect, they ransack your Berlin office and flat while you're away——"

" The balloon will, as you put it, go up," von Kressen shrugged his shoulders. " Well, if you have lived in hourly expectation of something for years, you can't complain when it happens at last."

" If it comes to fighting, there's the tank," Richards interrupted eagerly. " A light tank, Captain Loring, mounted with one of your own guns."

" By jove, is it!" Loring's eyes shone excitedly, as Richards went on to explain more precisely the presence of the tank in Germany, ending triumphantly: " and we've got it hidden in the forest, too, quite near here."

" It is a good idea," von Kressen said slowly. " If it comes to fighting, as Richards says, the tank would be very useful. We could pick it up on the way to the aeroplane hangar, although I'm afraid we can't carry it back to England in the machine."

" That won't matter, so long as she gets the chance of a bit of a scrap first," Richards said with a satisfied sigh. " She's dying for a fight, that tank. I'd have hated just to leave her parked there, not knowing what had become of us. Sorry—but I've a queer sort of feeling for that little tank," he finished apologetically.

Since there was no further reason for delay, von Kressen went to the door and sent one of the sentries with a message to the prison commandant. As he had expected, that individual accepted his explanation obsequiously, and sent an escort to take the prisoners out to the waiting car.

It all seemed almost too simple to be true. Von Kressen gave a few brief orders to the driver, whose upturned collar and down-turned cap almost hid his face, and they were off, speeding through the night in the direction of the forest.

As they went, it was decided that Richards and Shanks should form the tank's crew, after it had been retrieved from its hiding place. The car was stopped at the nearest point to the cache, and Jack went with the two others to help them bring the tank down to the road.

This was managed without difficulty. The tank had not been disturbed, and even in the semi-darkness was easily manœuvred for the short distance with the aid of an electric torch.

But on reaching the road and the car, they found von Kressen and Peter in a state of much anxiety and disturbance. They had been sitting in the waiting car and discussing matters. Absorbed in the examination of a road map, neither had noticed the precise moment when the driver had slipped out of his seat, but they became aware of the man's absence in time to see him running at full speed two or three hundred yards away down the road in the direction of Drachem.

As he crossed a patch of moonlight, he was plainly visible, and both men immediately realized that this was not their real driver and loyal accomplice, but a far shorter, more thickset individual.

" Muffled in the big coat and cap, it was easy enough for him to take his place, sitting in front of the car," von Kressen said. " But I ought to have made sure—it was madness to leave anything to chance, I'm greatly to blame."

" What do you think has happened?" Jack asked.

" I'm afraid there's no doubt about that. The Gestapo substituted one of their own men for our driver, in order to spy upon us, and he's gone back to report. Well, the hunt will only be up all the sooner, and we'd best get on quickly. Peter, will you drive? you know the road, so you'll have to lead the way. The tank must follow."

The small armoured column set out. Fortunately the road was good, and they were able to go at an average speed of some twenty miles an hour, though this was not by any means fast enough to satisfy von Kressen.

" We shall probably find the road blocked—be held up in some way sooner or later," he said. " The Gestapo authorities at Drachem will most certainly try to stop us— they'd be fools if they didn't—and nothing could be easier than to telephone to one of the military establishments along the route."

" Do they know the road we shall be taking?" Jack asked. " Had you given any instructions to this driver whom they'd substituted?"

" Only approximate directions—no details. Those were unnecessary, since my own chauffeur knew them and knew, too, that they must be kept entirely secret. But after we left the town I told him to take the Coblenz-Düsseldorf road and that tells them enough—too much! I curse myself for an idiot—after all my experience of Gestapo methods I ought to have been prepared for some such move."

He leant back in the corner seat, frowning and distraught. It was quite evident that von Kressen was in no mood to give any further explanations that night of the various mysteries which still needed elucidation. One could scarcely expect it in the circumstances, Jack thought philosophically. He felt uncomfortable enough himself at the mere thought of falling again into the hands of the Huns. But for von Kressen, who had for years systematically fooled them, foiled them, the prospect must be hideous—Jack had heard enough of Gestapo technique to realize that.

And the same thing held good for Peter; the youngster felt sure of that. Peter, who had been working with von Kressen, would certainly share in his fate, whatever it might be.

Gloomy thoughts enough, as they travelled on through the sombre, seemingly endless pine forests, the tall, sentinel-like trees black and in unbroken ranks.

The car's powerful engine purred almost noiselessly: in the rear, the tank ground its way along, rumbling and grumbling, full of complaints when they reached a stretch of road on the upgrade, yet plugging along indomitably.

Quite suddenly the car emerged from the forest on to open ground, the bald curved summit of a hill, covered with thin grass, out-cropping rocks and gorse clumps, all clear and distinct in the moonlight which seemed almost dazzling after the gloom of the forest. The road ran upwards for some distance, a pale ribbon, before disappearing over the crest out of sight.

" Almost at once it dips down into another wooded valley," von Kressen commented, " and that's where my machine is hidden in its hangar. Not more than four or five miles away now, but, contrary to the French saying, it's the *last* steps which count even more than the first."

The tank was still in the thick cover of the forest behind them, and could be heard labouring up the incline. Peter had just accelerated, to put on a speed for the run up over the hill crest when disaster occurred. It was preluded by a short snap, followed by a grating, grinding sound as the big car swerved sideways and came to a standstill across the road and almost blocking it.

Peter was out in a second to investigate the damage, while Jack ran back to fetch Richards from the tank. But after a short, although exhaustive examination, the faces of the two mechanical experts registered tragedy.

" I'm afraid there's nothing to be done, sir," Richards said dolefully.

" No," Peter agreed, shaking his head, " the gadget that is smashed couldn't be replaced except at a garage. It's a queer business, too."

" It is—looks to me very much as if the job had been done deliberately. It couldn't hardly have happened by accident," Richards declared.

" Sabotage, eh?" Shanks also had joined them beside the car. " Bit of dirty work at the cross-roads, engineered by that deputy-driver?"

" Probably," replied von Kressen. " Well, we shall have to leave the car where it is, if you can't get it going. Can we all pack into the tank, Richards? It's our only chance of reaching the hangar quickly."

" We could do it at a pinch, sir, though it will be that," Richards allowed. " It's a three-man tank at most normally."

" We must manage somehow. I feel sure there's not a moment to waste——" von Kressen broke off, listening intently. " Even now I fancy I hear something. . . ."

" I'll run up to the top of the hill and look," Jack volunteered. " Just to make sure the coast's clear."

He set off at top speed, but before reaching the crest, took cover, creeping from bush to rock, so as not to risk showing himself against the skyline. Raising his head cautiously, to peer through a gorse patch, there was at first nothing to be seen. Little more than half a mile ahead, the road, as von Kressen had said, plunged once more into dark pine woods and, up to that point, it was empty.

But a sound came from the forest, as though something stirred in the depths, the sound which von Kressen had already heard carried clearly on the still night air. Not the bird of the song . . . something far more sinister and deadly.

Even as Jack watched, waited, three black shapes emerged in single file from the trees, like great prehistoric animals coming out to browse on the sparse turf of the uplands.

Slowly, deliberately, they crawled into full sight. Reaching the open the two behind moved outwards, coming up on each side of the first, which kept on along the road. Twenty-ton tanks, with projecting gun-muzzles defiantly raised, they advanced slowly up the slope, as formidable a road-block as a tiny opposing force can ever have faced.

Jack was already racing back towards the group round the broken-down car. He told his news breathlessly, and von Kressen nodded.

" Just as I expected," he said. " We shall have to rely on the tank to get us away and out of this hole, although it's rather a forlorn hope."

" I don't know so much about that, sir," Richards broke in eagerly. " Don't forget we've Captain Loring's new gun on the tank, with its projectiles. They're not expecting that."

" They're not expecting anything like the tank itself for that matter—they think they've only the car to deal with, don't they?" Jack pointed out. " That would be a very easy thing to tackle, and when they find it broken down, they'll fancy the job will be easier still. . . . I say, couldn't we lead them into a trap—an ambush . . . keep the tank back where it is, well hidden among the trees, and when they come along to mop us up, believing we're all still in the car, *then* we'll open fire and scupper them."

Jack paused, more for lack of breath, than for want of ideas which rushed into his mind as he evolved the plan.

" By jove, I believe it might work," Peter said. " Anyway, it's worth trying. Don't you think so, von Kressen?"

" I think it's a good idea," von Kressen answered gravely. " But we must get back to the tank at once. Much depends upon making them believe we are still hidden in the car and at their mercy. We want to draw them close to the trap, if we're to catch them."

Somehow or other, they all managed to pack into the tank, although, as Richards remarked, it was a real work of art.

" Not that I care, so long as I've got elbow room enough to work the gun when it's needed," he said. " Mind you, I don't say that we'll get her best speed out of the old lady, if it comes to a get-away, overcrowded like this. Anyway, it's a good thing we brought her along, isn't it? I always felt in my bones that she'd bring us luck."

A queer interval followed, which seemed far longer than it actually was, as they waited in the close darkness of the tank, enclosed in the denser dusk of the forest. Ahead, framed by the tree-trunks at the road's opening, they could see the black shape of the derelict car, athwart the track: beyond, the rising slope, pale in the moonlight.

For some moments there was silence, broken only by the whirring cry of a nightjar, answered by its mate in the distance. Then, once again, came the menacing thunderous sound of the grinding tank-tracks on the hidden farther slope.

Suddenly, the three monsters heaved themselves up and over the hill-crest and halted there again, while presumably their hidden crews surveyed the scene before them.

CHAPTER XVI

Three to One

" The lull before the battle, eh?" Shanks murmured. " And like all great strategists, we should try to guess the enemy's thoughts."

"Not much doubt about those," von Kressen said. "They think we're ambushed in the car, and they are planning how to make us surrender."

"Do you think they will open fire from the tanks?"

"No. They'll certainly have been given orders to take us alive if possible. Dead, we're of very little use to the Gestapo. At the same time, the tank crews won't be particularly keen on the job of tackling us; they know we'll be armed—and pretty desperate customers into the bargain."

"I wish they'd make up their minds and get down to it," the Irishman grumbled. "I hate being held up—kept waiting for things to happen."

Jack felt much the same. This was somehow an inhuman sort of affair.

Those three motionless tanks made a battle picture so different from those of his dreams, which remained a schoolboyish medley of scarlet-coated ranks, firing volleys, charges and generals with their staffs, however unlike real modern warfare he knew all this to be.

To Shanks, trained only for the winged swiftness of air fighting, these armoured monsters were fantastic, fairy-story things like the dragons challenged by knights of old. Or, possibly, skipping a thousand centuries or so, ultra-modern highway robbers, calling on travellers to stand and deliver.

As far as Richards, a practical soldier, was concerned, they were just Armoured Fighting Vehicles, a fraction of the modern battle front, of which he thoroughly understood the workings.

"Look, they're moving!" he said, peering through the tiny slit in front of the driver's seat.

Slowly, majestically, the three tanks ground their way down the slope and halted again nearer to the car.

From one of them came a stentorian voice, shouting in

German, a sound that was most uncannily discordant, breaking in on the stillness and peace of the moonlit scene, where such murderous tragedy might soon be enacted.

"They're calling on us to surrender to avoid useless bloodshed, aren't they?" Jack said.

"Yes—although it's only *their* blood presumably," von Kressen answered. "We ourselves shan't be very tenderly treated if we fall into their hands, I can assure you."

"If you do not immediately give yourselves up, we shall fire!" the same harsh voice proclaimed.

"They won't," von Kressen remarked drily. "Not until they've investigated the car—and found that we're not in it."

"You cannot deceive us. We know that you are there," the voice broke in so appropriately that Shanks laughed.

"Hear him! Doesn't it sound like the 'Fee—fi—fo—Fum! I smell the blood of an Englishman?' Pity we can't do something about it, if they reconnoitre the car, before the time comes for using our heavy armament on the tanks themselves."

"We might—we've got the Bren gun," Jack suggested. "If that was taken out of the tank and hidden behind those bushes over there, it would enfilade anybody coming nearer to the car, and draw off their attention *and* fire in that direction, too."

"It seems a sound idea," Peter said. "What do you think, von Kressen?"

"So long as the machine-gun isn't used until they're quite satisfied we're not in the car—yes."

The Bren gun accordingly was carried over to the spot which Jack indicated. He and Shanks were detailed to serve it, a duty which at any rate provided a very welcome change from the canned atmosphere of the tank. But they were not allowed to enjoy the freshness of the night air in peace long.

They had scarcely established themselves in the thicket with their weapon before there were movements on the part of the enemy.

Five men emerged from the middle tank, carrying Tommy-guns and grenades, and began to approach the car stealthily, spreading out so as to surround it. Shanks chuckled under his breath as he watched these proceedings. It appealed to his sense of humour that such excessive precautions should be expended upon an empty car.

One of the Germans, an under-officer, taking the lead reached the side nearest to the tanks, slightly before his comrades, and shouted another demand for surrender before thrusting his head and a raised grenade through one of the windows.

Next instant he fell back, with dropped jaw and staring startled eyes.

" No one here! They are gone!" he cried, and the other four soldiers at once joined him, crowding round the car, peering into and under it, before they seemed to have thoroughly made up their minds that it was empty.

Then, in their disappointment, they gave an exhibition of spite and rage, which, but for its ugliness, would have been almost grotesquely childlike. They slashed at the car with trench knives, kicked it with their heavy boots, smashing the glass of the windows, slitting the cushions.

This senseless destruction might have gone on, but for a sudden clatteration, like that of a big typewriter, and a sharp pit-a-pit-a-pat-pit-pit of bullets, peppering the bonnet and roof of the car.

The German tank crew were taken completely by surprise when thus attacked from the flank. One of them fell, huddled on the car's footboard, at the first burst of Bren-gun fire: another was wounded in the thigh, and dragged himself away groaning painfully.

The rest scattered in consternation, withdrawing at top-speed to the shelter of the tank. There followed a rapid barking interchange of orders; then the guns of the tank on the right of the three were traversed and depressed to aim in the direction of the thicket from which the Bren gun had fired.

"Thud—thud!" and then the heavy crash of the missiles among the trees. There were spurts of yellow fire as though the dragon-like monster was breathing flame from its nostrils.

But those missiles fell harmlessly as far as the Bren gun and its crew were concerned. They had already removed their weapon to another position now that the first phase of the fight was finished, and were consulting with the rest of their force.

"We've stopped the tank crews for a bit, from trying to nose us out," Jack said. "They won't care to make any further investigations under Bren-gun fire, I fancy."

"No, but it isn't any use against the tanks themselves," Peter pointed out. "And this delay is only giving the Gestapo more time to concentrate on our tracks. We ought to get away as soon as possible—even if we leave the tank and try to reach the aeroplane-hangar on foot."

"Ah, don't let's do that, sir," Richards begged. "Not until we've given your gun the chance to clear the way for us. It can do that and more."

"You're optimistic," Peter Loring shook his head. "The gun's had no real test yet: it's an unknown quantity."

"That's all you know, sir," Richards said darkly. "Just give me a fair show. I don't ask for more."

The three tanks had drawn closer together, as though in consultation. There was something ominous in the movement: a joint bombardment might be contemplated, Jack pointed out.

"And once they really opened fire together, I don't see how we—or the tank—could escape," he said.

"No, you're right," von Kressen answered. "It seems that if this new gun of yours is to come into action, now is the time—or never."

"And they're a beautiful target, all bunched together like that," Richards murmured exultantly. "Couldn't ask for a squarer deal—at close range too."

He was loading and manipulating the gun as he spoke: perhaps the least nervous of the little group, just because his task was the most absorbing and important. Jack's hands felt cold and clammy; he had a horrible sinking sensation internally, and Peter's white strained face told him that he must be feeling much the same.

They were staking so much upon the happenings of the next few minutes. If the gun was a failure, it would be not only a disappointment, but a disaster, as far as their present desperate predicament was concerned. How small and unimpressive it looked, to be able to do what was claimed for it! And in the event of disappointment its use would only have exposed their whereabouts to the Germans, and they could scarcely hope for time to escape, before the combined fire of the enemy tanks smashed on to them.

"I'm ready, sir," Richards said, his eyes gleaming as he turned them upon Peter Loring. "It's for you to give the word."

For a moment Jack thought, watching him, Peter seemed almost inclined to refuse. Then he set his jaw and nodded grimly.

"Very well," he said. "Are we all set? Ready for whatever happens?—and heaven knows what that may be! Then—FIRE!"

The report which followed was surprisingly soft and muffled. Jack, who had forgotten that this was one of the outstanding peculiarities of Peter's new invention, was taken aback and all the more unprepared for the next happenings.

The projectile hit the centre tank fairly and squarely amidships, and immediately there was a dull, thudding explosion, with a cloud of peculiar blue-grey smoke, flecked with crimson, which rose and spread fanwise. This was followed by a violent sizzling noise and dazzling out-bursts of reddish-green flame, licking voraciously in all directions, like the tongues of great beasts of prey.

As the smoke-cloud cleared, it showed an amazing sight. There had been no violent rending explosion, but the big tank was disintegrating, falling to pieces. . . . Lumps of metal and armour-plating dropped from the fabric of the huge machine, the mighty caterpillar tracks sagged out-wards, as the deadly acids released from the projectile ate into the metal, riddling and destroying all the substance of which it was made.

The dark shape of a man struggling to extricate himself showed for a few seconds against the terrible unearthly glow, then fell back and disappeared.

Richards fired again. The elevation of the gun was rather too high this time, and the projectile struck the turret of the tank on the left, but the result of the shot was the same— a shattering, a dismembering, as the tongues of flame licked up, down, and all sides. Above, a lurid glow lit the night sky, as if cast upwards from the mass of embers in an enormous dying fire.

A remnant of the two tanks' crews had managed to escape alive from that shattering destruction, and as the fumes and smoke partially cleared, these fugitives could be seen scrambling away, most of them obviously badly hurt. Shouts of alarm and confused orders came from the sole remaining tank and its crew began to fire wildly, so much so that the shots had no effect, although they tore through the trees in unpleasantly close proximity to the British force.

"With any luck, we'll knock out all three," Richards muttered, as he prepared for his third shot—perhaps over-confidently, as things turned out.

For this time he only scored a near miss, even if it removed the danger of a successful attack by the third tank, and its now completely panic-stricken and demoralized occupants, who stayed for no more interchange of shots.

Groaning and grinding, it was turned in its tracks and lurched away up the slope, followed by a parting shot from Richards. This ripped along one side of the tank, scarring and injuring, without actually disabling this last of the enemy fighting vehicles. But Richards was bitterly disappointed with his semi-failure.

"Rotten bad marksmanship," he grumbled at himself. "I *ought* to have scuppered all three of the blighters. Can't think what made me mess up things like that. One thing—it wasn't the gun's fault, in any way."

"Oh, come, you didn't do so badly!" Jack laughed excitedly. "In fact, you put up a grand show, didn't he, Peter?"

"Why—why, I can't say much at present," Peter, indeed, looked a trifle dazed. "It's rather disconcerting to find one's own invention so much better than one expected: takes a bit of getting over."

Sparks from the burning tanks, or the shots from the enemy guns, had started fires in the dry forest growth around and behind the British party and clouds of pungent, choking smoke rolled out over the open ground.

"This is getting a bit too hot to be pleasant," Shanks said. "Isn't it time to get a move on?"

"It certainly is. Start her off, Richards," von Kressen said. "The way's clear now—at least we'll hope so."

The little tank seemed bent on showing off her paces as well as her fighting power and so justifying Richards' high opinion. She started as easily as a Rolls-Royce, and emerged from the forest to roar up the slope.

It was necessary to make a fairly wide detour to avoid the burning ruins of the gun's victims, and when they reached the crest, it was to see the third enemy tank just lurching out of view along the track into the farther forest belt, for all the world like a wounded elephant or buffalo seeking cover, as Jack said, remembering adventure stories of big-game hunting.

" Yes—and almost as dangerous a customer if it is fairly driven to bay," Peter Loring answered. " I know Richards is itching to run down and finish them off, but we've not enough time to spare."

" Seems a pity to let them go," Richards owned. " When they're only just ahead."

" Ahead they must remain, till we've reached that point in the forest where we turn off," von Kressen said. " It's our only chance of escape."

It was a strange race for life which followed, with those who should naturally have been the pursuers in front instead of behind. For the German tank-crew were certainly trying their hardest to escape from the intended victims of themselves and the Gestapo, who, in their turn, were making no attempt to overtake them, as they left the open hill-crest and entered the forest again.

A real mix-up, Jack thought, sitting cramped in the tank's dark interior, although this " Black Hole " ordeal did not last for long.

After some fifteen minutes, von Kressen from the conning-tower gave the driver of the tank a brief order.

" We're nearly there, Richards—stop just beyond that next sharp bend."

Richards obeyed—and as he swung round the corner and came to a grinding standstill, von Kressen uttered a fierce imprecation.

" Look at that !"

" What cursed luck !" Peter Loring muttered. " Didn't I say a badly wounded tank might be as dangerous as a buffalo ?"

There, scarcely a hundred yards away, where the track took a steep upward gradient, the German tank also had halted, obviously broken down, for a couple of the crew were outside, working frantically to repair some damage to the track sprocket.

Two white terrified faces turned towards the British tank: arms were raised, with cries of " Kamerad !" which were echoed from inside the vehicle. It was plain that the Nazis expected Peter's gun to open up again and were anxious to forestall it by giving themselves up.

" We can't be bothered with them," von Kressen said in English, then addressing the would-be " kamerads " in their own language: " Stay where you are. We don't want to take you prisoners, and we won't hurt you if you obey my orders. Remain inside the tank, until we are out of sight: if you move before that—if you make any attempt to follow us, we shall open fire at once."

A chorus of frightened voices promised obedience, the two Germans outside scrambled back into their tank and von Kressen turned to other considerations.

" We've reached the end of this stage of our journey: we have to abandon the tank now. We must leave it here and slip back, round the bend, before we enter the forest, so that they won't see exactly where we go, what direction we take."

Richards' face fell as he looked from one to the other of his companions, imploring sympathy.

" Leave her here," he repeated woefully.

" Well, we obviously can't take a tank with us in the aircraft. We shall be overcrowded in any case," von Kressen said. " I'm sorry, Richards—but there it is."

" Then I'll put her out of action," Richards declared. " *They* shan't have the use of her anyway—she'd hate that worse than anything."

" Can you do it quickly?" von Kressen asked. " While we're getting out the machine from the hangar?"

" I'll make it only a matter of minutes, sir," Richards assured him.

" Then come with us and I'll show the way, so that you can follow."

The others had slipped out of the tank and were collected in a group round the bend in the road, concealed from the eyes of the Germans in the other vehicle. Now they all followed von Kressen as he led them to a particular spot in the dense thicket of rhododendrons which here skirted the track.

" As you see, there's no apparent break," he said. " Nothing visible from the road. . . . But if you take this bush with the curiously twisted trunk as a sign-post, slip round it and pull aside these low branches—there!"

A foot-wide path appeared, well defined for all its narrowness and leading straight through the thicket.

" Follow that and you can't miss the way," von Kressen told Richards. " It'll take you direct to the hangar, about a quarter of a mile farther on."

" Right." Richards waited for no more. The rest followed their leader in single file, sometimes bending double, sometimes almost crawling, as the tiny secret path drove through the high shrubs, like the game trails in a jungle.

Without warning they emerged into a cleared space, level and grassed over, but with bushes here and there, breaking up the surface. On one side was what appeared to be a rambling ruined cottage, a low wooden building, with the most completely desolate and unlived-in look, as though it had been empty for years.

Von Kressen, however, gave a low whistle, and a man came out from this building. He had a square, resolute face, very grim, until he saw von Kressen and smiled with obvious relief.

" Ah, gnädige Herr, you've managed to get away," he said.

" Hardly yet, Michel—you're looking too far forward—but there's a good chance of escape. This is my mechanic, Michel: you can all of you trust him, as I do absolutely. He's utterly dependable, and hates the Nazis even more than I do myself if possible—with good reason! Michel made this clearing and built the hangar with his own hands; he has kept the machine for months ready to start instantly day or night. Isn't that true, Michel?"

" It's true. She is ready," the mechanic answered.

" And you're ready to come with us?"

Michel nodded. He was evidently a man of few words.

" But where is the hangar?" Shanks asked perplexedly.

Von Kressen laughed.

" A good bit of camouflage, eh? Yes, that ruined cottage, no less. The whole front is a canvas screen; behind is the hangar. Open it, Michel, let them see. And then we'll help you to bring out the machine."

Michel was already dragging aside the camouflaged screen, with its realistic door and windows framed in creepers. Inside the dark aperture the tilted nose and winged shape of the aircraft could just be distinguished.

" But I say," Shanks was looking round with an expert flyer's eyes. " We can't start off from here—all those bushes——"

" Camouflage again," von Kressen told him. " Show him what you do with the shrubs, Michel."

The mechanic obeyed by simply picking up the nearest bush, a low thick-growing juniper and carrying it bodily away to the side of the clearing.

" They've no roots, you see. Well, are we ready? Because, if so, the sooner we're in the air the better."

" I say, Richards hasn't come back," Jack cried in consternation. " I wonder what's happened to him. He should have been here by now."

" He certainly should—and we daren't wait much longer. After all, I have to think of the safety of the *whole* party," von Kressen said.

" I'll run back and look for him." Jack started at once without waiting for opposition or protest. It was impossible to leave Richards like this, even if it meant returning to the trap himself. But he did not have to go far. Half-way to the main track, he heard a puffing and blowing, the scrape of something being dragged with much difficulty. There was Richards, crimson and perspiring, hauling along a bulky object which almost blocked the narrow path.

" I couldn't leave this behind for them to take, Mr. Frere," he panted. " The captain's gun—what a mercy it is easily dismounted and no heavier. And there are ten rounds in this case. They may be useful yet."

" Richards, you're mad, you know, but you're a marvel! However did you manage to get it away under the very noses of the Nazis?"

" Put the fear of God into 'em," Richards grinned. " They're so afraid I've got the gun set up somewhere among the trees, that they won't go near the tank for a long time. Anyway, she's out of action."

With Jack's assistance, the precious gun was conveyed to the aircraft without much further difficulty, and although

von Kressen and Michel looked grave over the extra weight,
they agreed that the weapon might be useful.

Thanks to the special device which was one of the gun's
novel features, it could be mounted so as to make firing
practical from the rear cockpit.

Shanks took his place at the controls: Michel started the
engine, and clambered in as the machine began to taxi
along slowly. The night had passed to its end almost unnoticed, and it was into a pink, dawn-flushed sky that the
aeroplane mounted, circling, banking, skimming low over
the trees.

" We've made it!" Jack drew a long breath of relief.
" We're well away."

" Don't be too sure." Peter, pressed close beside him,
was staring downwards. " This is still German sky, remember, and—look!"

CHAPTER XVII

A Land-fall

The German tank was now almost immediately below
them and, hearing the aircraft, its crew had come out and
were staring upwards, talking together excitedly, pointing
and gesticulating.

Then, after a hurried consultation, one of the men began
to run away from the stranded vehicle along the road.

" Gone to give the alarm—tell the authorities about our
get-away," Peter said. " And it won't take long to send up
fighters from the nearest airfield to intercept us."

" No," von Kressen calculated. " Meisburg aerodrome
is only about ten miles away, as a machine flies. If they find
a telephone, it may be only a matter of minutes. We haven't
much of a start."

When the news was communicated to Shanks through the speaking-tube, he thrust out his chin like a battleship's prow and nodded with determination.

" Then the quicker we're off the mark the better," he returned. " There aren't going to be any clouds either, so we can't play pussy with 'em."

The sky, indeed, was too clear to provide the slightest cover. As they rose higher, the whole of Germany seemed spread out beneath them, looking, Jack thought, exactly like a colossal sand-table. He picked out von Kressen's hidden airfield and hangar, for instance, so easily that the value of the uprooted bushes, removed by Michel, as camouflage, could be plainly seen.

" The only wonder is it wasn't discovered before," he said. " Surely somebody must have noticed something?"

" Probably questions would have been asked," von Kressen answered. " If it hadn't been under the secret protection of Hitler himself . . . in an underhand way. He actually gave me facilities, provided one of his own aircraft. . . . You see, he wanted my help as a possible messenger to other countries and governments if need arose —if he saw a chance of saving his own skin in an emergency. . . . He trusts nobody—suspects everybody, even himself. I sometimes think his plan is to set all those around him against each other. . . . He hates them to be real friends: it must be just a pretence. The plan works, I suppose . . . up to a point." Von Kressen spoke intermittently as the machine flew north-westwards over Germany, with dawn-light flooding the sky, gleaming here on the course of a river, there on the windows of a building. Now and then a flight of birds showed against the pale, gold-suffused blue, looking much like distant aircraft.

And then, staring at one such V-shaped flight, Jack realized that this time, these were neither wild duck, rooks

or seagulls, but real machines—fifteen Messerschmitt 110's,
flying out of the sunrise, following their trail. There was
no need to point them out to Peter or von Kressen: they
had already seen.

"As I expected, they didn't take long," von Kressen
said. "And I'm afraid this machine isn't fitted either to
race them, or face them."

"No, the chances look poor enough." Peter spoke quite
dispassionately, as one who had foreseen this probability
for a long time. "And, personally, I'd rather crash into the
North Sea than into the hands of the Gestapo, if it's a case
of devil and deep sea. I wish it didn't involve these
youngsters though—and poor old Richards."

The sea was no mere figure of speech. They were nearing it now; it stretched away to the horizon, a vast tray of
beaten metal, gleaming in the sun, fringed at the edge with
white, where waves broke upon beaches.

But this was no moment for admiring seascapes, when,
all the time, that birdlike flight of aircraft was gaining upon
them—steadily gaining.

"They're overhauling us," Peter said gravely. "In a
few minutes, they'll be swarming round. What are our
chances with regard to baling-out, von Kressen?"

"Two parachutes and a rubber dinghy intended for two.
We never foresaw more than a brace of fugitives, you see, and
so kept all the equipment as light and compact as possible."

"And the two who are to take those chances?" Peter
asked, and the eyes of both men met in a level glance.

"I'm sure you'll agree with me as to that, Loring?" von
Kressen answered. "The two youngest, of course."

But those two youngest members of the aircraft's crew
thought differently when the parachute-harness was passed
over to them.

"Hey, what's this?" Shanks questioned. "Umbrella,

eh? 1 thought I heard there weren't enough to go round. If not, I don't need one, thanks very much all the same."

Jack, when approached, was even more positive. " I won't put it on," he said doggedly. " You and Mr. von Kressen are the ones who ought to get away, Peter, if anybody can. The rest of us don't matter."

" Of all the obstinate young cubs! The only thing to do then is to draw lots, von Kressen—these two won't obey orders. Where's my match-box?"

When the lots were drawn, the two short matches fell to Richards and Michel, a result which made Jack grin.

" So providence didn't agree with any of our little arrangements," he said. " Never mind. Perhaps none of us will want to bale out."

This transaction had only been a matter of minutes, but by now the German machines were very near and dividing up from their compact clustered formation into small sections, each of which then moved forward in single file, one aircraft close behind the other.

It was plain enough what these manœuvres meant. They planned to surround the British machine on all sides, above and below, rather as crows or jackdaws mob a strange bird which has invaded one of their colonies. Afterwards, they could close in and bring their guns to bear from any and all directions.

They were right over the sea now, flying at such a height that the few vessels in sight appeared like tiny black water-beetles on its surface.

And now Shanks took command with the natural authority of the trained fighter, the old gladiator, who knew his element, his machine, all the technique, tactics and strategy of air battle. There had been no consultation: the others took it for granted, when he gave his orders to Richards, as the air-gunner, through the speaking-tube.

" Let 'em have it with the machine-gun as soon as one comes within range. We want them to think that is our only armament: then they'll be even bolder than odds of fifteen to one ought to make 'em! But as for the new gun, hold your fire with *that* till the very last minute, till you can practically see the whites of their eyes and feel absolutely certain that you've got 'em. Now, I'm going to play them for all I'm worth—show them the tricks of the trade. So good hunting!"

Shanks proceeded to carry out this intention in a game of catch-as-catch-can, with the sky as playing-field, a game as elusive, as tantalizing to the enemy as anything could well be.

But the Germans were still closing in, and now the whine of shells from one or other of the Me.s mixed with the roar of the conflicting machines.

The dog-fight was well and truly under way now. Richards sat tense and expectant, getting in, every now and then, a well-directed burst of machine-gun fire. So far, the Jerries had scored very few hits, although several cannon-shots had passed unpleasantly close, and there were many near-by explosions which rocked the plane. But, on the whole, the enemy were still playing for place, over-confident at first that they could bring matters to a finish at their own chosen time.

Consequently, at intervals they retired, reformed and advanced again, giving a narrower target and with obviously growing impatience to finish off the affair.

It was during one of these concentrated attacks that a single Messerschmitt roared in, so close that it looked as though her pilot meant to ram the British machine.

At the last instant, the German flyer changed his intention, and by bad manœuvring passed broadside on, across the tail of the other machine, so giving Richards his long-waited opportunity.

It was then that the German flyers, like the tank-crews before them, got the surprise of their lives. Expecting no more than that machine-gun fire which was the only defence hitherto put up by the fugitive aircraft, they had no idea that it was armed, metaphorically, to the teeth.

Richards fired, and the shot struck the Hun's tail-plane. There was the same dull impact, the same outburst of strangely coloured fire, pale now in the bright sunshine, the same licking flames.

And then the aircraft simply fell to pieces in the air, a shattered mass of chunks of burning material.

Shanks, at the controls, had difficulty for a few moments in steadying the small aircraft, tossed and shaken as it was by the violent displacement of air caused by the explosion. A German machine, following immediately behind its leader was caught by a falling wing-strut, swerved, turned turtle, and went down in a spinning nose-dive to crash in the sea.

And now Shanks saw his own chance to attack. Turning, he drove the machine straight into a German formation of three, bringing her into position for Richards to get in his second shot.

This caught the leading German amidships, as the pilot jinked and banked to avoid a collision. Once again, the instantaneous result was immediate and complete destruction and within five minutes Richards had sent down another two.

The effect on the other Huns was demoralizing, and their shooting became as wild as their tactics. Two of them tried to surprise Shanks by a combined rush from different directions, firing cannon and machine-guns alternately. But the Irishman used avoiding action and the projectiles whined beneath his machine harmlessly.

After Richards had succeeded in adding a fifth and sixth Jerry to his bag, the enemy had obviously had enough.

Five minutes later, nine Messerschmitts could be seen streaking back towards Germany at a speed which must have been almost a record. Another five minutes and the sky was as empty as the sea, which stretched beneath as seemingly calm as though it had been smoothed out by some great rolling-pin.

All the visible movement in the universe seemed centred for the moment in that one small aircraft flying steadily homewards, battle-scarred, but still fighting-fit.

Shanks gave a sigh of relief and satisfaction, and spoke through the tube.

" O.K., Richards?"

" O.K., sir," Richards responded wiping the perspiration from his forehead and the palms of his hands.

" Kite's all right, eh?"

" Not much wrong, sir. Hole or two here and there."

" Gun's all right, anyway—*and* the gunnery."

" Thank you, sir."

It was the two experts communing together. Even Peter Loring, the gun's inventor, felt at that instant as though he had had very little actual part in the victory.

But what, after all, did it matter? The victory was won, and the machine set on a straight course for England. That was the only thing of importance, and so felt each and every one of that strangely assorted airborne sextet, so totally different mentally and physically, yet linked together in such close association.

To Jack every beat of the engine throbbed " England—England—England—" as if the plane itself repeated the word as it sighted that yellowish-white streak stretched along the horizon, like an oasis in the desert of the sea.

Then they were above land once more, patchworked in brown and green, purple of clover fields, yellow of mustard, with the dark lines of hedgerows, the pale streaks of roads.

All so homely, so natural, so English: Jack felt as though he had been exiled for years, rather than for—how long was it?

Good heavens, surely it could not be only thirty-six hours or so, since the Whitley bombers with their loads of commandos had left the airfield? It seemed utterly incredible that so much had happened in so absurdly few hours.

Jack knew enough of the lie of the land to realize that Shanks was making for the home station of his squadron.

Well, that seemed the natural and reasonable thing to do. Oddly enough, not one of the six in the aircraft detected the possible flaw in the procedure.

" My word, I could do with a good breakfast in the mess," Shanks spoke in Jack's ear. " It's my treat—What shall we order? Sausages—kippers—eggs and bacon—kedgeree—toast and marmalade. . . ."

" All the lot, I should think—for us all?" Jack laughed. " I don't feel as if I'd had a square meal for a year."

" They'll be jolly surprised to see me back," Shanks chuckled. " I shall have been marked off as a pukka crash. Now, watch me! I'm going to make the best landing of my life."

" How about a Victory Roll?" Jack suggested.

" One for each of those six Hun kites? No, no, I hate ostentation. I was always a modest bloke. Besides, it was Richards, not me: I'll leave him to do his own rolling. Hullo! What the—how the—why the——"

The Irishman ended with a splutter of incoherencies, and for a second Jack thought that he must have suddenly lost control of the machine.

Then, all of a sudden, a second machine seemed to materialize from nowhere, and sped past with dartlike swiftness. There came a staccato rattle, followed by the sharp patter-patter of machine-gun bullets against the wings and fuselage.

A Spitfire—for a few seconds Jack was utterly dumb-founded, before he realized the truth.

Theirs was a German machine with German markings complete, the Swastika, the Iron Cross—nothing whatever to show that it was not an enemy nuisance raider, prying round the airfield. Of course, a British machine had come up to drive them off. What else could be expected?

Von Kressen and Peter had already seen what was amiss and saw, too, what an extremely ugly situation had developed.

They had no means of communicating with the ground station, no wireless installation which would serve tne purpose of establishing their identity, no way of signalling which presented itself immediately.

And Shanks in his fury at the attack seemed scarcely capable of realizing that the other pilot's mistake was quite natural, that he could scarcely be expected to act otherwise.

"Takes us for a Hun, does he?—that's no excuse!" he spluttered furiously through the tube. "He's no right to—ought to show more sense. Why—why, it's Tubby Filmer, too, chap I've known for years—in my own flight, the dirty blighter! Ah, *would* you!"

The Spitfire had swooped down upon them again, all guns blazing and spitting, and the duel continued, Shanks, in spite of his blinding rage, manœuvring the machine with wonderful skill in order to avoid the other's fire. But it was scarcely a time to appreciate such skill, expecting as they all did, to be brought down in flames at any moment.

What an end to their adventures to die in a dog-fight with a British plane! No wonder Shanks saw red.

Round and round the landing-ground, the two machines circled, dived, banked. Quite a crowd had gathered about the hangars and work-shops, to stare upwards, and Peter and Jack began to scribble hasty messages on sheets torn from their notebooks, to be thrust into a cigarette-case, secured to a wallet with an elastic band and dropped, in the forlorn hope that one of these communications might be picked up in time.

Richards, too, had somewhere discovered a large piece of cardboard and printed upon it in big letters: "We're all British!" This he was holding up and waving in vain attempts to attract the pilot's attention.

A fresh outburst of fire from the British machine was followed by a cracking, splitting sound, as the other plane lurched over sideways in a sickening manner.

"Hit—something carried away!" Peter exclaimed, and simultaneously came the Irishman's grim voice through the speaking-tube.

"That's torn it; I can't keep her in the air. I'm going to try a crash landing—stand by, all of you, in case it doesn't come off."

Down went the machine's nose, tilted at an absolutely incredible angle, seeming as though it must inevitably plunge straight into the tarmac which appeared, rising to meet them at a most alarming rate. But in the last split-second, Shanks miraculously flattened out. The aircraft just touched ground, skidded along on the under-carriage, bounced once or twice, then subsided sideways upon the crushed and crumpled wing, but so perfectly handled that there was no crash, no explosion.

Except from the pilot—and he made up for all such lack in the machine's behaviour.

Tumbling out of the cockpit, Shanks stamped, shook both fists at the Spitfire, which was still circling gracefully overhead, shouted up at the sky and its occupant, his brogue rising to boiling-point as was usual with him on these occasions.

"Och, come down out o' that, ye murderin' omadhaun!

But you daren't! You know only too well what's afther waitin' for yez whin ye set fut on dhry ground!"

He swung round on the swarm of ground mechanics and other staff who were now running up from all directions to surround and apprehend the supposed German airmen, who had made a forced landing.

"An' phwat do *you* want?" he demanded. "Aren't yez ashamed of yeselves, standin' gaping an' makin' a show ov' us—and you wid not the exuse of himself above there, who might well be proud of the chanst to fight wid wan who's more than his equal in the air. Not that I'm takin' anny excuses from Tubby Filmer—he ought to have known bether, so he did, settin' on us and——"

"Why, it's Mr. Ryan!" one of the mechanics shouted, provoking another outburst from The O'Morough-Ryan.

"An' who else should it be? Would ye have me goin' round wid a sky-sign? Amn't I known here well enough widout bein' obliged to do the likes of that, if I'm not wishful to be set upon an' shot out av the sky by a lot of airway gangsters, no less. . . ."

By this time the other members of the party were surrounded by interested and excited questioners, and had imparted enough information to clear matters up. Jack was recognized and welcomed by several of the airfield's personnel: messengers were sent to headquarters and wireless communications transmitted to Flight-Lieutenant Tubby Filmer, still sky-patrolling.

As a result, this individual landed, shortly afterwards, and came hurrying across to soothe the irate Shanks, an unwontedly sober expression on his usually round and chubby face.

"I say, old chap, I'm most awfully sorry," he apologized. "But no one gave me the gen—how was I to know that you were piloting that bandit kite?"

" An' phwere else would I be?" Shanks demanded with dignity. " Sure, 'tis not what I would have expected from you, Tubby, to be thryin' to pinch a gong by bringin' down an ould friend in flames on me own airfield."

" Now, you know, I didn't know all there was to know!" poor Tubby protested ungrammatically. " I wouldn't have shot *you* down for anything in the world, Shanks."

" Well, well, it was a good fight an' I don't mind telling you I'd have been sorry to miss it." Shanks was grinning now, his eyes placid and blue as the sky. " I'll forgive ye, Tubby—if you'll take us all to breakfast and make sure that there's plenty of sausages and bacon. I promised it to them, ye see."

CHAPTER XVIII

Jack keeps an Appointment

Meeting once again the steady steel of Colonel Parker's eyes, Jack Frere caught a kindly flash from their greyness, as though sunshine had struck a drawn blade.

This time he was not alone with the colonel. All those who had escaped from Germany with von Kressen were present, except Michel, the mechanic, whose lack of English would have made the proceedings quite unintelligible to him.

" Well, gentlemen," again the colonel's eyes glinted. " We've got a great deal to hear and to tell which, of course, mustn't go beyond these four walls. All the same, I think these three—" his glance swept Jack, Shanks and Richards —" have earned the right to hear as much as they don't already know, and to ask any questions they like, which I will answer as well as I can."

"I think you had better begin by giving them a character sketch of myself," von Kressen said. "Otherwise they may well be still doubtful as to which of my various impersonations is the real man!"

"Very well. I'll introduce the genuine Max von Kressen to them then—Anti-Nazi, Anti-Hitler, anti-everything those names represent, secret agent, in the German Reich, of Great Britain with the Allied nations—and one of the bravest men I know."

"Come, come, don't talk such nonsense, my friend," von Kressen said. "Anyone who loves his country is naturally willing to work to save it from gangsters, that is all—even if, incidentally, he risks his life to do so."

"You did that every day and every hour you lived in Germany."

"Well, it was my job—*our* job, eh, Loring, and I'm not sure that your part was not even harder than mine," von Kressen said gravely. "For an officer in the British army to act the part of a traitor, that can't have been pleasant."

"So definitely *un*pleasant"—Colonel Parker's voice was very quiet—"that I hesitated for a long time before asking Captain Loring to undertake it. And it is to his credit that he accepted the task without hesitation."

Jack, listening, felt all the old hero-worship of his cousin returning, only increased many thousandfold. He had never faltered in his own loyalty to Peter, always believed in him—and how thankful he was to remember that now!—but, for a time full understanding had been impossible, though not trust.

And, of course, even now he did not know or understand everything; eagerly he waited for Colonel Parker's next words which promised light on the matter.

"I suppose Mr. Frere and the others haven't heard yet just what your work entailed, Loring?" he said.

" No, sir. I didn't feel free to explain without your permission."

" In your capacity as XX77. . . . Very well, I'll give them the facts." And the colonel proceeded to do so in a calm, matter-of-fact manner.

Yet the story he told in those brief sentences was so amazing that it would scarcely have been believed, Jack thought, if set down in a boy's adventure book, so perfectly correct it is that truth outdoes fiction.

As Jack already knew, Peter was, like von Kressen, a secret-agent, although unlike the German, also a professional soldier. The two had not actually met before that day when Jack encountered them upon the stairs at Lamorna Mansions, although Peter had heard much from Colonel Parker regarding von Kressen's extraordinary career and unique position in the Reich, working against the Nazi party from his place in its very centre.

It was von Kressen on one of his visits to England who had actually suggested to the colonel the plan which Peter was chosen to carry out, partly because of his knowledge of the German language. Like many other great schemes, it was as simple as it was daring, when put into plain words, this idea of Loring acting, as the renegade " Captain Peter ", a second "Lord Haw-Haw", delivering the most venomous broadcasts from Germany in English, which, all the time, concealed vital information, sent daily in this way to the British Secret Service over the air.

" The code of letters and words we used was very secret, known only to me and a deputy, and we changed it occasionally for the sake of safety," Colonel Parker said. " I'm not going to give actual examples, but as an instance those broadcasts given by ' Captain Peter ' a few weeks ago, apparently only sneering at what the Germans believed to be our invasion plans, actually gave me by means of our code the most precise details of Hitler's intentions—which he unfortunately cancelled at the very last moment—of spending the night at Schloss Schwartzigen, before the meeting at the Drachem Sports Stadium."

" It sounds as easy as possible told like that," Jack said. " But——"

" Ah, yes, that ' but '," Colonel Parker smiled. " It covers a lot—all the hairbreadth escapes, the vigilance, the fear of the tiniest slip, which might give the whole thing away and mean not only instant death, but complete failure. And all the time, the knowledge of being hated and despised by both sides alike, I imagine, Loring, that must have been the worst of it."

" It was . . . pretty bad," Peter said. " But it doesn't matter now."

" It was so terribly bad that he doesn't want to talk about it or even think of it," Jack guessed, watching Peter's face. He made an effort to change the subject, to switch it away from his cousin.

" What I can't understand, sir," he said, addressing Colonel Parker, " is how Herr von Kressen managed to go backwards and forwards as he did between Germany and England, with no interference from the authorities on either side. It seems so strange."

" It was only possible because he was provided with papers and passports by *both* sides," the colonel answered. " Hitler's own secret police were chuckling to think how completely hoodwinked we were in England, how we believed Hitler's own personal henchman and envoy to be an innocent neutral motor-salesman, or whatever it was he happened to be representing over here. And, all the time, when he was on British soil, he was under observation by the inmost circle of the C.I.D.—and under the protection of a more secret body still."

The explanations went on. They heard how one of von Kressen's errands, a matter very dear to the Führer himself had been the plan to steal or secretly buy the plans and blue prints of Peter's Anti-Armour gun and projectiles, rumours concerning which had leaked through to the German Great General Staff even before the outbreak of war.

Von Kressen had used this to cover certain other schemes and to stage the kidnapping of Peter Loring, carried through by means of an aeroplane provided by Hitler which had been given secret facilities for landing in England, and returning to Germany, by the authorities on both sides.

But he had already discussed the broadcasting plan in several interviews with Colonel Parker, and the code by which information was given had been arranged and handed over to Peter by the colonel himself.

Once Peter was in Germany, it had been easy for von Kressen to point out to the Nazis the advantages of using him, since he was willing to betray his country, in the interests of the Reich. It would have a great effect on public opinion if a serving British officer broadcast to England— and every word which he was to speak would, of course, be submitted beforehand to Dr. Goebbels and his propaganda department, for their censorship and approval.

" So both sides were satisfied," von Kressen said. " But it made it necessary for me to take several journeys backwards and forwards to England. That time, for instance, when you handed over the secret file to me, Mr. Frere—so very reluctantly! There was a revised code for the broadcasts in it, as well as certain not over-correct details concerning the gun, for Nazi consumption only."

" Yes, I could see Mr. Frere was being very worried indeed over that affair," Colonel Parker said. " In fact,

I'm sure he thought that I was taking serious matters much too lightly and snubbing him badly too."

"Oh, no, sir, that would have been awful cheek," Jack reddened. "It was only——"

"I know exactly how you felt, and it did you credit. I was only sorry that I couldn't explain—then. Well, I think we've cleared up things in general now: I shall be seeing you again later in the day, von Kressen, about our new schemes."

After leaving Colonel Parker's quiet room, the five paused on the pavement of Horse Guards' Avenue to exchange a few final words before separating.

"Do you know what your next work is to be, Loring?" von Kressen asked.

"Well, I've got a few days leave first. Jack and I are going to spend that in Surrey, telling each other all our adventures." Peter smiled at his cousin. "And, after that, I'm going to have a real rest."

"That's good hearing! Where, may I ask? I hope it is what the last war called a cushy job."

"Somewhere at the Front, I hope, eventually anyway, when training is finished. They've given me a regiment: it's to be fully equipped with my own anti-armour guns," Peter said. "Richards is coming with me too, as an instructor; he's had so much practical experience and made such fine scores that I couldn't wish for a better man."

Richards beamed with delight, then glanced at Jack apologetically, as though afraid he would be offended.

"It isn't that I'm not more than sorry to leave you, Mr. Frere," he said in deprecating tones: "but I can't pretend it won't be great for me to go back again to work for the captain. You wouldn't expect me not to feel like that, would you?"

"I shouldn't believe you if you said you did, and I'd be

ashamed of you, too," Jack answered. " As for Shanks and myself, we've nothing with half so much kick in it to report. We'll just be going back to our old jobs, as far as we know."

" You must, all the same, have got a certain amount of excitement lately, even out of such humdrum occupations as flying and commando raids!" von Kressen laughed. " I couldn't wish you more thrills and variety surely?"

" No, I suppose not," Jack looked doubtful. " But——"

" *But* we don't often come in for that sort of thing," Shanks grumbled. " Usually, flying's just as monotonous as walking. I was going to ask if you couldn't give me a job in your own line of country, Mr. von Kressen?—unless, of course, *you*'re making a change too, retiring so to speak to another job of work."

Von Kressen shook his head gravely, rather sadly.

" No, I'm afraid not," he said. " I must go where I'm most use, which means staying nowhere for long and going everywhere or anywhere, sometime."

" Then you'll be off again soon, sir, and I don't suppose you can tell us when or where?" Jack said.

" No. Because I don't know myself, for one thing."

" But it won't be Germany again surely? That would be impossibly dangerous, even for you, after what's happened," Jack urged.

" Perhaps for that very reason, because they won't expect me, I may be wanted there," von Kressen said quietly. " But it won't be, next time, as Hitler's right-hand man, I can safely promise you that!"

" We shall hear from you?" Peter asked. " At least, you'll write sometimes."

" I can't promise even that, but you'll hear *of* me, perhaps. As you know, Loring, the kind of job I've taken on, which you're fortunate in escaping from, is a lonely one. Possibly after the war, we who stand here now, shall meet again. I hope so. You've been fine comrades: the best a man could wish. For the present then, good-bye—and good luck to every one of you."

They all shook hands. Then, acting on a sudden impulse, the four from whom von Kressen was parting, stood simultaneously and rigidly at the salute, until that unobtrusive figure in the well-remembered brown suit, had rounded the corner of the Avenue and passed out of sight into the thronging crowds of Whitehall.

"There, as Colonel Parker just said, goes a very brave man," Peter Loring spoke first. "As no one knows better than I do. I could never have carried the job through without him, and what this country owes to Max von Kressen will never be understood until after the war—perhaps not even then."